"I'd like to talk to you about Petey,"

Taylor said nervously. "You were right, Matt. He is lonely."

Matt liked Petey and felt the little boy reaching out to him. He didn't doubt Taylor was doing all she could, but it dawned on him that Petey wasn't used to his aunt's privileged lifestyle.

Taylor said as much. "Petey's had a life of baseball, games, playing in the park. Everything is so different for him with me." Too much was at stake not to be candid. "I—I'm not sure how to be a parent."

So she needed a man's touch in Petey's life, and she'd picked him.

"Would you be willing to spend time with him?" she asked. "Of course, I'd be willing to pay you."

"I'll spend time with the boy," Matt said gruffly. "But let's get something straight. I won't take your money."

Suddenly Matt saw her beautiful eyes light up, and he wondered just what he'd gotten himself into....

Dear Reader,

Welcome to Special Edition…where each month we publish six novels celebrating love and life, with a special romance blended in.

You'll revel in *Baby Love* by Victoria Pade, our touching THAT'S MY BABY! title and another installment in her ongoing A RANCHING FAMILY saga. In this emotional tale, a rugged rancher becomes an instant daddy—and solicits the help of Elk Creek's favorite nurse to give him lessons on bringing up baby.

And there's much more engaging romance on the way! Bestselling author Christine Rimmer continues her CONVENIENTLY YOURS miniseries with her thirtieth novel, about an enamored duo who masquerade as newlyweds—and brand-new parents—in *Married by Accident*. And you won't want to miss *Just the Three of Us*, Jennifer Mikels's tender love story about a high-society lady and a blue-collar bachelor who are passionately bound together for the sake of an adorable little boy. Then an estranged tycoon returns to the family fold and discovers unexpected love in *The Secret Millionaire* by Patricia Thayer—the first book in her WITH THESE RINGS series, which crosses into Silhouette Romance in September with *Her Surprise Family*.

Rounding off the month, Lois Faye Dyer will sweep you off your feet with a heartwarming reunion romance that results in a surprise pregnancy, in *The Only Cowboy for Caitlin*. And in *Child Most Wanted* by veteran author Carole Halston, a fiercely protective heroine hides her true identity to safeguard her nephew, but she never counted on losing her heart to the man who could claim her beloved boy as his own.

I hope you enjoy these books, and each and every novel to come!

Sincerely,

Karen Taylor Richman
Senior Editor

Please address questions and book requests to:
Silhouette Reader Service
U.S.: 3010 Walden Ave., P.O. Box 1325, Buffalo, NY 14269
Canadian: P.O. Box 609, Fort Erie, Ont. L2A 5X3

JENNIFER MIKELS

JUST THE THREE OF US

SPECIAL EDITION®

Published by Silhouette Books

America's Publisher of Contemporary Romance

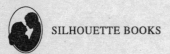 SILHOUETTE BOOKS

ISBN 0-373-24251-4

JUST THE THREE OF US

Copyright © 1999 by Suzanne Kuhlin

Printed in U.S.A.

Books by Jennifer Mikels

Silhouette Special Edition *

A Sporting Affair #66
Whirlwind #124
Remember the Daffodils #478
Double Identity #521
Stargazer #574
Freedom's Just Another Word #623
A Real Charmer #694
A Job for Jack #735
Your Child, My Child #807
Denver's Lady #870
Jake Ryker's Back in Town #929
Sara's Father #947
Child of Mine #993
Expecting: Baby #1023
Married...With Twins! #1054
Remember Me? #1107
A Daddy for Devin #1150
The Marriage Bargain #1168
Temporary Daddy #1192
Just the Three of Us #1251

Silhouette Romance

Lady of the West #462
Maverick #487
Perfect Partners #511
The Bewitching Hour #551

JENNIFER MIKELS

is from Chicago, Illinois, but resides now in Phoenix, Arizona, with her husband, two sons and a shepherd-collie. She enjoys reading, sports, antiques, yard sales and long walks. Though she's done technical writing in public relations, she loves writing romances and happy endings.

PETEY'S INSTRUCTIONS FOR CONSTRUCTING A NEW FAMILY

Step 1: Move into your terrific aunt's humongous house.

Step 2: Be extranice to Lottie the cook so she'll bake lots of yummy cookies for you.

Step 3: Play hide-and-seek with Leeland the butler, pretending he's your playmate.

Step 4: Become best buds with the cool carpenter, Matt, when he helps you build a tree house.

Step 5: Jump for joy when Aunt Taylor invites Matt along to do fun stuff.

Step 6: Act real proud when your awesome aunt becomes your Little League team mother.

Step 7: Don't snicker too loudly when you catch Aunt Taylor and Matt snuggling.

Step 8: Hope with your whole heart that someday the three of you will be one big happy family....

Chapter One

"You're worrying about Petey, aren't you?"

Standing at the open terrace doors, Taylor Elmhurst smiled over her shoulder in response to Sarah's question. Why had she thought she could hide anything from the person who'd been her best friend since they were nine and performing pirouettes in ballet school? "He's so young and so vulnerable, Sarah. I don't want to make any mistakes."

Sarah's large, brown eyes met hers. "Petey loves you."

That he did was what made her ache. Since he'd come to live with her, Taylor had realized that he had a problem, and she didn't know how to solve it.

"Aren't making mistakes part of being a parent?" Sarah continued, obviously beginning to have doubts about attempting parenthood herself if it was so difficult.

"I suppose so." Taylor hadn't thought she was ready for a child. Then, overnight, she'd become guardian, parent, the only family to her five-year-old nephew. The newfound relationship sometimes scared the daylights out of her. But except for her nephew's propensity for early wake-ups, she loved having him with her. At the sound of movement behind her, she turned away from the doors and the view of the pool and the flower garden. "Do you want something to eat?" she asked as her butler, Leeland, set a tray of croissants and scones on a side table by Sarah.

"Maybe a scone." Sarah brushed back her bangs. Her long brown hair trailed down to the middle of her back, and it was usually clipped back or twisted up. Today she wore it in a French braid. "Other people don't seem so uptight about raising kids, Taylor."

"Other women have nine months to adjust to the idea of being a parent." She settled on an adjacent sofa and poured coffee for both of them from the silver coffee server. "Then they get to make little mistakes with babies, like using the wrong baby bottles or securing a diaper improperly. I have a person here." A sweet, wonderful person. "I don't want to do anything that will traumatize him."

Most of her life Taylor hadn't had to think about anyone else. She'd been single. Spontaneity had been part of her life. On the spur of the moment she would leave for Europe. If she felt like lounging in bed all day, she simply rang a bell and Leeland brought her a tray of food whenever she wished. If she felt like staying out until sunrise with a date or not coming home, she followed her whim. Now she had to answer to someone else. True, Petey was a little boy, but he would be anxious if she wasn't there when he awakened in the morning. And she could hardly yank him out of school to dash off somewhere. No, her life was different suddenly. She was a parent. And she had no idea how to be one.

Sarah hissed as she dropped crumbs in the lap of her orange silk pantsuit. "Did I tell you about Buffy Morrell's latest?"

With no answer in sight to her problem, Taylor gave her friend her attention. "The gothic-looking guitarist from Sweden?"

"No, he was last week. This one is—"

"Aunt Taylor!"

Petey's panicked yell jolted both of them to their feet.

His shirt halfway out of his pants, his blond hair mussed, he burst into the room from the open terrace doors. "You gotta help. My cat's stuck." Tears welled in his blue eyes. "It went into the really big tree by the flowers," he said, gulping his words with his excitement.

Adrenaline no longer pumping through her at a laser pace, Taylor crossed to him and placed her hands on his shoulders. He'd been so withdrawn for weeks after his parents' death. Only recently, after she'd purchased the cat, had a light come back into his eyes. "Shh," she soothed, kneeling before him. "We'll get Echo down."

Sarah stepped closer and touched the top of Petey's head. "Of course we'll get it."

Taylor swiveled to look back at her, surprised.

"*You'll* get it," Sarah said quickly, and shrank back as if evil faced her. "You know that I don't climb trees." This from her oldest friend, the one who'd pledged her blood to Taylor when they were nine years old.

Seriously, she'd known her friend wouldn't ruin the designer original she'd bought in Paris two weeks ago. And the last time Sarah had broken a nail she'd stayed home from a luncheon until she could get her nail repaired at the salon.

Having stood quietly nearby until then, Leeland asked, "Shall I call the fire department?"

A week ago, Taylor wouldn't have thought twice about such a suggestion. But on the previous weekend, she'd personally learned the importance of firemen being free to respond to fires. She could still recall arriving home to a gray fog of smoke near the garage, to the sight of the fire engines parked in helter-skelter fashion on the front drive of her estate, to the maze of hoses snaked across the immaculate lawn, and she'd been grateful for the department's quickness. She'd only lost the garage and not her home. No, she wouldn't bother the fire department. "Is the gardener still here?"

"No, miss," Leeland answered. "But the carpenter is."

Keeping Petey's hand in hers, Taylor went with him out the terrace doors toward the garden area.

He turned pleading blue eyes up at her. "You'll get Echo, won't you?"

Behind them, in a shuffling run, Leeland suggested, "I could get the ladder, miss."

Then what? She would never reach the cat from the ladder. And she certainly couldn't ask a seventy-year-old man, a loyal and devoted employee to climb a tree. For Petey's sake, she'd already asked Leeland to do several tasks that had stretched his physical capabilities, like playing catch. No, he couldn't do it.

"Taylor, you aren't going to climb the tree." Sarah sounded so aghast that Taylor nearly laughed.

She tossed a you've-got-to-be-kidding look over her shoulder at Sarah. Taylor Elmhurst did not climb trees—never had. Her mother would not have indulged her daughter through a tomboy phase.

"Mommy or Daddy would," Petey piped in.

Taylor felt her heart sink. She'd been trying so hard to keep him from missing his parents too much.

"You'll get her, won't you?" Petey asked again.

Intimidated by a five-year-old. She ran a multi-million-dollar company. At twenty-nine, surely she was confident, intelligent, capable enough to make a decision about how to rescue a small cat.

As they approached the tree, she saw the black-and-white cat, curled on a branch as if paralyzed, and meowing loudly. Near it in a sweat-soaked, snug T-shirt and equally tight, worn-looking jeans, a man balanced on a tree limb.

Sarah's voice purred with interest. "Who is that?"

Taylor didn't know, but he was drop-dead gorgeous. No other thought came to mind. Dark hair, long and shaggy, fluttered beneath the wind's caress. His face was angular with high cheekbones and strong, square jaw. Fascinated, Taylor watched muscles flex, noted the sheen of moisture on his suntanned arms as he descended the tree with the cat in his arm.

For a long moment she studied him, almost to the point of rudeness. A woman wouldn't forget that face. She was certain she knew him. Or had seen him before. But where? "Who are you?" she asked the moment his sneakered feet touched the ground.

He turned a toe-curling smile and his gray, deep-set eyes on her. "The carpenter."

"My carpenter?"

Faint lines crinkled at the corners of his eyes. "If you say so."

Distracted, as she tried to place him, she let the humor slide by. "What is your name?"

"Duran." He pivoted toward Petey and eased the cat into his arms. "Matt Duran."

Sarah inched close enough for Taylor to feel the heat of her body. "What time is the dinner party tomorrow night, Taylor?" she asked as an obvious excuse to get noticed.

Taylor barely focused on her question, and Sarah, she knew, couldn't have cared less. Without another word, the man being ogled turned around and headed back to work.

Slowly Sarah released a long breath, her eyes still riveted to Matt Duran's tight backside in those snug-fitting jeans. "Now, *he* is simply delicious, Taylor." She sighed exaggeratingly. "Too bad he's poor."

Taylor cocked a brow, drawing a short, amused laugh and a shrug from Sarah. ''I meant that we can hardly grab just anyone, even if he is tall, dark and handsome. Do you know what my mother would do if I brought him home?'' Sarah imitated her mother's haughtiest tone. ''No pedigree, darling.''

Taylor slanted a look at her. ''Let's go in. You've already spent too much time contemplating the man.''

Me, too.

She looked exactly as Matt remembered her. Delicate and small-boned, she was more angles than curves. A leggy beauty with a fluid walk that had caught his eye five years ago. He'd seen Taylor Elmhurst at a high-society party. Her arm had been hooked with that of an Ivy-League type. Wearing something ice-blue, soft and flowing that had clung to her slim curves, she'd looked like a princess. Overhead lights had shone on her soft blond hair. Chin-length, it had swayed with her movement when she'd laughed in that smoky-sounding voice.

Back then he'd been living in a penthouse apartment, and had enough money that, if he'd wanted to, he could have romanced her royally. At that time in his life, he'd been successful in the construction business and living in a different world, and Alisha had been in his life. Since then, he'd lost not only the business he'd worked hard for, but also the woman he'd thought he loved. He was back to square one, rough calluses on his hands again.

Realistically his blood had never been blue enough for a Taylor Elmhurst. More importantly he knew now she wasn't the kind of woman he wanted in his life. She was part of a different world. But he would never deny that there had been instant attraction, then and now. And he wondered if he was one of those idiots who knew when something was bad for him and still gravitated toward it.

Reaching into his truck, Matt jabbed at a button on the CD player. Faith Hill always soothed him. He let the music blare away to accompany the hum of the saw.

Beneath several silver oak trees, near what used to be a triple-car garage that had burned down, he'd set up a work area with sawhorses and his tools. Beyond the rambling, Spanish-style house and its landscaped lawn stretched the Arizona desert of stunted yellow grass, its flatness broken now and then by a cactus or a wispy bush, continuing as far as the eye could see.

Often during the past few days, Matt had seen a hawk circling for prey, or spotted a jackrabbit hopping between distant straggly desert shrubs. With the air warm, but not hot yet, he enjoyed the outside work. He would be finished with the job before the heat of late spring began, before the desert turned toasty.

Whistling along with the music, he finished making a cut. Only then did he notice the boy standing near and watching him.

"What are you making?" The kid, about five and darn cute with his sandy-blond hair and blue eyes, inched closer. Thin, all limbs, he smacked a ball into a baseball mitt.

"I'm rebuilding the garage."

"We had a fire," he said helpfully.

Matt smiled. "I know."

"And lots of firemen were here." He pushed a toe of his sneaker into the soft dirt. "I might be a fireman someday."

Matt measured another board. "That's a good thing to be."

The boy's pale brows bunched. "Or a wrestler. I really like wrestling." He raised thin arms and flexed them. "Or I could be a ninja."

For the boy's sake, Matt kept laughter out of his voice. "Yeah, you could." He picked up the saw, then set it down, deciding his work could take a backseat for a few moments. "What's your name?" he asked, sensing the kid was in need of company.

"My name is Peter, but my aunt calls me Petey. That's better, I guess. Thank you for saving my cat."

Matt decided not to mention that the cat would probably have taken care of itself if left alone. "You're welcome. The blond lady is your aunt?"

"Uh-huh." He craned his neck to look over Matt's tools. The questions Matt expected flowed from him. "What's that?" he asked, pointing at a cordless drill, then at a level. "What do you use this for?"

Silently the kid cried for male companionship. It didn't take much for Matt to recognize the boy was hanging on to his every word as he answered the questions.

"My dad had one of those," Petey said, indicating a circular saw.

Matt heard sadness in the young voice and focused

on him, wondering what had started it. "Did you use it?"

"No." He looked down. His toe dug deeper in the dirt. "He promised someday that I could but..."

Disappointment, resentment, sorrow. Matt heard it all in the boy's voice. The light had left his eyes.

"Aunt Taylor said he went to heaven. Mommy, too."

Matt knew the look in the boy's eyes would haunt him. He'd known pain, too much for someone so young. Unlike some kids, Matt had had a good life, great parents. His father had taken him fishing and to football games and ice skating. He'd known birthdays and holidays filled with laughter and love. He couldn't imagine being alone at such a young age.

Certain the boy's loss was fairly recent, he thought about letting him help hammer some uprights tomorrow. Keeping him busy might help. But to do that he'd need the aunt's okay. Oh, hell, maybe he should mind his own business.

Looking up again, he saw the boy plodding away toward the house, kicking up dust with the toe of one foot. Matt drummed up a quick reminder. The kid wasn't his problem. He had his aunt, and with her money, he could have anything.

At dusk Matt stopped for a fast-food dinner of a burrito and a taco before driving home. Home was a small studio apartment behind his shop in a strip mall. In the alley, Matt unlocked the building's steel back door. He entered a square-shaped room he used as a weight room, with a bench press, a treadmill and a rowing machine.

Munching on the burrito, he ambled through the small kitchen. In passing, he dropped the bag dangling in his hand into the trash can. He could have lived elsewhere, but he'd chosen the convenience of living behind his shop. He didn't mind the cramped quarters. After Alisha, he'd relied on work to get him through some angry days.

The feel of wood beneath his fingers gave him pleasure, ranking second only to the softness of a woman. At sixteen, he'd been a carpenter's apprentice, working after school and on weekends. He'd gotten the job because he was the boss's son; he'd kept the job because he'd worked his tail off. His father wouldn't have had him any other way.

By the time Matt was twenty-four, he'd had years of experience. He could have stayed in Ohio and eventually taken over his dad's company, but he'd branched out on his own, coming to Arizona where the building industry had been thriving. Within three years he was owner of Duran Builders, one of the city's most successful construction companies. Eighteen months later he was buried in debt and had lost his company. With hard work he knew he could get it started again, but did he want to? That was the big question.

He stepped into his shop, a garage-size room at the front of the building, and stopped beside the mahogany breakfront he'd been refinishing for an acquaintance. Almost done, it gleamed with its original gloss and beauty.

Behind him, he heard the opening of a door, then

felt the coolness of the April breeze. He turned to see his sister, Cara.

Dressed in black tights, lavender leg warmers and an oversize sweatshirt—attire for the health club where she worked as an aerobics instructor—Cara moved near. "Pretty," she said, touching the breakfront.

Matt settled his backside against the edge of a round table and finished off the last of his burrito. "Aren't you working?"

"I'm on my way there." Wandering to the rolltop desk in a corner, she shook her dark head, then poked at a button on his answering machine. "Why have this, if you don't check your messages?"

Matt gave it a cursory glance, wondering when she planned to tell him the reason for her visit. "I forget it exists."

Dimples cut into her heart-shaped face. "You're impossible." She pushed the button.

Grinning at her, he listened to the message. A female caller, Lannie Esten, left her phone number and a request that he call her.

Cara sent him a questioningly look. "Who is she?"

"Don't know her."

"So did you take the new job?" she asked with a nonchalance he didn't buy.

Though five years younger than him, she'd always played mother hen. "Quit worrying."

"Alisha—"

He raised a halting hand. Because of what happened to him, she had a tainted view of the wealthy. "Forget Alisha." From the beginning of his affair with her, his sister had harped at him with a standard cliché that oil and water don't mix.

"Did you meet her?" she asked, aware the name Elmhurst appeared often in the society column.

To avoid a lengthy explanation about her, he gave an answer that he hoped ended his sister's questions. "The butler hired me for the job." He dabbed a napkin at his mouth. "I'm rebuilding the garage. A fire leveled it." He recalled the thin, elderly man moseying into his shop. Leeland was Mr. Proper. And Lottie, the cook, a short and ample-figured woman who possessed a steady stare that dared anyone to give her trouble, was sometimes as earthy as a dockworker. They were quite a pair. Amazingly, because of a huge dose of mutual respect, they seemed to work well together.

"Are you going to that ball game?" Cara swept a hand toward the desk where he'd dropped the tickets for a baseball game, a thank-you from one of his neighbors for repairing a back gate.

"Want the tickets?"

"Wish I could take them, but I'm going to a George Strait concert. Find some kids," she said on her way out. "And call Mom. She's fussing about you."

He waited until the door closed behind her, then headed back to the kitchen for a beer. He popped the can before he settled on a chair. With the receiver cradled between his jaw and shoulder, he stretched to reach the television set in a corner of the kitchen counter. He knew a kid who would probably love to go to the game.

He punched his parents' phone number. Instead of a greeting, he got the answering machine message. From the television, canned laughter accompanied the dialogue of a popular sitcom rerun. Matt stared at the screen with unseeing eyes. His mind provided a stronger image. Long after he should have set down the receiver, he still held it. He couldn't forget the look in the kid's eyes when he'd mentioned his father.

Chapter Two

Though heavy, pewter clouds crowded the sky, threatening rain, Matt had arrived on the job at seven that morning, hoping to cram in a few hours of work before it began. Despite the gloominess of the day, only a drizzle came down. It started, then stopped fifteen minutes later.

Restless for no real reason, he strolled toward the house to take advantage of an invitation Lottie had made days ago. Come to the kitchen anytime. He wondered what she'd baked this morning, already hooked on her blueberry muffins.

At the back door, he reached for the doorknob, but didn't turn it. Through the door's window, he saw the boy eating his breakfast. The kid looked miserable…lonely. Matt recalled seeing the aunt, in a gray power suit, leave at seven-thirty that morning.

As he opened the door, the boy looked up from running the spoon through the milk. Matt thought about some spare lumber he'd planned to discard. "Want to build a fort?"

"I don't know how."

"I'll show you. Come on." Matt reasoned that he drank too much coffee, anyway. He could do without a cup or two. "We'll get the wood together now and make the fort when you get back from school. Okay?"

A smile finally lit the boy's face. "Okay." He pushed back his chair and rushed to Matt.

"I'll have coffee later," Matt said to Lottie.

Before he closed the door, he saw the woman's wide grin and heard what he guessed was her way of expressing approval. "I'll save a slice of apple pie for you."

Nothing was going well. Awakening late, Taylor had been rushing since her feet touched the floor. Earlier, she'd come out of the bathroom to find Petey and Echo sitting on her bed, waiting for her.

The look in Petey's eyes had made her want to call in sick, but she'd had an appointment with several board members and had needed to go to the office. She understood Petey's insecurity. She was all he had left. She assumed that it would take time for him not to feel a little scared when she was away. Before leaving him, she'd promised they'd go to a movie tomorrow. He'd nodded, but the smile she'd longed to see on his face hadn't formed.

Now, her stomach growling for lunch, she gave up

any pretense of working. Unsettled, she swiveled her chair away from the highly polished cherry-wood desk and toward the panoramic view out the window of the Phoenix skyscraper.

On a cloudless day she could view the Camelback Mountains from her twenty-sixth-floor office. Three times a week she drove in to the city to work. Since her father's death, she'd taken over the helm of Elmhurst Properties, which included apartment, industrial and business complexes. She'd always been goal driven, career oriented. That had pleased her father, but now she needed to make time for Petey. Balancing motherhood and a job wasn't easy.

Instead of reviewing a quarterly report, she couldn't stop fretting. She made a call to home, knowing the chauffeur would have picked Petey up from kindergarten by now. She wondered if he'd eaten lunch yet. Was he watching his favorite afternoon cartoon—the one with the bulldog? Mostly she wondered if he was sitting alone somewhere.

Before she asked a question, Leeland offered reassurances that dinner was being prepared.

Taylor closed her eyes. She prided herself on her organizational skills and excellent memory, yet she'd forgotten about the dinner party, a thank-you to several of the contributors who'd helped make a money drive for a women's shelter successful. "Leeland, is Petey in the study watching television?"

"No, miss. He's outside."

Guilt instantly washed over her as she surmised that Petey had pleaded with Leeland to play catch with him. It wasn't fair to ask a man of his age to include such exerting tasks in his daily schedule. "You were playing baseball again?" she asked while making a notation on the report in front of her.

"Actually, no, miss." He sounded so relieved.

"He's playing alone?"

"He's with Mr. Duran. The carpenter."

She stilled the pen in her hand. "What are they doing?"

"Master Peter is hammering, miss."

Hammering? "Thank you, Leeland." Frowning, she ended the call. She sort of understood Petey's attraction to the man. He was probably filling a void. But what if Matt Duran wasn't thrilled to have a little boy hanging around? A less-than-sensitive person who viewed Petey as a pest might be too blunt and hurt him badly.

"You look preoccupied."

Lost in thought, she'd been oblivious that Martin Calin, the company's general manager, had even entered the room. He was in his late fifties, a thin, tall man with a serious look who had a tendency to peer over the rim of his wire-rimmed glasses.

"I'm sorry, Martin. Have you been waiting there for very long?"

"Not long." He smiled with an understanding that she appreciated. "Is Peter all right?"

Taylor managed a more convincing smile as he settled on a chair across the desk from her. "Yes, he's fine." Considering his recent loss, he seemed happy enough, but Taylor sensed something wasn't quite right. Keeping the thought to herself, she led Martin back to the business at hand. "Did you do the market analysis of the area around the apartment complex on Wiletta?'' She'd thought the investment might become more valuable when a new ballpark was built.

''Already done.'' He bent his head and withdrew papers from a manila file folder he'd opened on his lap.

Taylor appreciated Martin. He was always efficient. Without him, she'd have been lost during the weeks while she'd dealt with the funeral, the sale of Jared and Elizabeth's small house and Petey's move into her home.

Petey. She couldn't stop thinking about him.

Somehow she managed to finish the meeting with Martin and hold a conference with the board members, but immediately afterward, she gathered papers needing her signature, then hurried to her car. Being home with Petey suddenly seemed more important. She wanted so badly to do everything right. After what he'd been through, he deserved someone who didn't fumble and blunder.

By three o'clock, she was negotiating her car onto the private drive that led to the security gates of her home. She removed the remote from her purse and entered the code to open the gates. On the seat beside her, her cell phone rang. Before she picked it up, she hit the button to stop the CD player and the soft lulling notes of Celtic music.

Sarah rushed a hello. ''I'm in a hurry, but I had to call and find out if he had sent you flowers yet.''

The *he* was Ian St. John. In what Taylor viewed as a showy display of affection, whenever she had guests coming, Ian sent her flowers. Of course, her women guests oohed and aahed about the romantic gesture, which is what Taylor believed was Ian's real purpose in sending the flowers. "No."

Laughter laced Sarah's voice. "He is so—so obvious."

"He wants to get married." Ian was the one her father had chosen for her. In fact, eight months before his death, he'd introduced her to Ian. "He's intelligent, successful, the right sort," she said to Sarah.

"The wrong one for you."

"Is he?" she asked, passing through the gates and wheeling the car along the drive to the house.

"If he wasn't, you'd have said yes by now."

Taylor said nothing, her attention shifting to Petey. Sitting on the hood of Matt Duran's truck, his legs dangling, he was chattering enthusiastically. Had he been with Matt all afternoon?

"Why so quiet?" Sarah questioned. "Is something wrong?"

"Nothing." Taylor steered conversation toward details about a bridal shower for a friend. By the time she'd parked, they'd decided on a restaurant and made plans to work on a menu and guest list next week.

"I have to go," Sarah said more brightly. "I have an appointment at Roth's for a massage."

"I'll see you this evening." Taylor said goodbye and tucked her phone in her shoulder bag. Stalling, she stood beside the car and watched Matt Duran. Head bent, shirtless, concentrating on the boards he was sawing, he gleamed with perspiration.

Moving closer, she could hardly ignore the rock-hard muscles in his arms and his back, or the flat plane of his stomach. But drooling over him wouldn't do, she reminded herself.

As she walked toward Matt and Petey, a twig snapped beneath the sole of her pump. Almost in unison, they both looked back at her. Taylor's stride faltered slightly as disconcerting gray eyes collided with hers. She was imagining nothing, she knew. She'd have had to be blind not to see the message of distrust. But why? she wondered instantly. He didn't even know her.

"You're home," Petey yelled.

As he rushed to her, Taylor opened her arms to him, certain now she'd been right to leave the office early. She was going to ask why he hadn't changed out of his school clothes, but she noticed the note pinned to his shirt.

"I got this note. You have to read it," he said with urgency. "It's for a field trip. We're going to a museum. Can I go?"

Taylor smiled at his excitement while she unpinned the note. Because she'd barely gotten a smile out of him for several weeks after his parents' death, she now treasured this childish exuberance. "Well, let me read the note. Then I'll let you know."

"Okay."

Sure the note could be signed at some later moment, she slid it in her purse. "Why don't you go in the house now." She took his hand. "You shouldn't bother—Mr. Duran."

"He said I could call him Matt," he was quick to tell her.

"If he's imposing—"

She looked all business in the gray, tailored suit and pale blue blouse. Matt shook his head, stopping her. Sunlight played across her face, casting the edge of her lips and the curve of her jaw in shadow.

"What's 'posing?" Petey asked.

"What you're not doing," Matt assured him, looking away in response to the sound of a truck engine.

Taylor turned to see a delivery man emerging from a florist's truck and nearly laughed at how predictable Ian was. There would be a dozen roses and a card with no message, just his name.

"I found my snake, Aunt Taylor." Petey dropped his baseball in his mitt, tucked it under his arm and dug with his other hand into a back pocket of his jeans, then withdrew a foot-long wiggly, plastic green snake.

Not thrilled, Taylor offered her best smile. Why did little boys like creepy things?

Noticing the look on her face, which was more of a grimace than a smile, Matt veiled a grin. He recalled owning a plastic black spider. At seven his favorite pastime had been dangling that spider over his unsuspecting cousin's head. The day was complete when she screamed bloody murder.

"I used to have one of those," he said about the snake.

"Just like this one?" Petey asked, sounding impressed.

"Almost."

Taylor wasn't surprised. Though it was fleeting, she'd caught a gleam of devilment in Matt's eyes when Petey had shown her the toy snake. She touched Petey's shoulder. "Didn't Lottie make chocolate chip cookies?"

He danced the snake in front of him like a yo-yo, then shoved it back in his pocket. "Do you like chocolate chip cookies, Matt?"

The boy was a delight, Matt decided. He gave him a thumbs-up gesture. "I'm a big chocolate chip man."

"Yeah. Me, too." Petey mimicked, "I'm a big chocolate chip man, too."

Hero worship, Taylor guessed. Relief coursed through her, now that she knew she wouldn't have to deal with Petey's hurt feelings because of rejection. "Why don't you get some of them?" she suggested to him.

He angled a pleased smile up at her, then turned it on Matt. "Do you want some, Matt?"

"No, but thanks."

"Okay. Maybe tomorrow," he said, revealing his usual optimism.

Matt smiled after him. A friendship of sorts was beginning with him. He liked the boy. He was also curious about him. "Both of his parents are dead?" With her nod, Matt realized that he'd assessed everything accurately. The kid had been through far more than anyone his age should endure. By the sadness that flashed in Taylor's blue eyes, he realized that she, too, had suffered. "Sorry. Your sister or—"

"My sister-in-law and brother." Taylor felt an unexpected catch in her throat and sucked in a quick breath. How long would it take before she no longer felt as if she was choking when she said that?

"That's tough."

"Especially for Petey. He kissed them goodbye before going to school. On the way to pick him up later, their car reached an intersection at the same time as a lawyer's. He'd been celebrating a courtroom win with a liquid lunch and ran the red light."

A brittleness had hardened her voice. She'd had a difficult time, too, Matt guessed.

Taylor resisted the grief. She'd gone through the stages of mourning rapidly. She'd had little choice. Because she'd had a child to care for, she'd had no time for denying the deaths, or wrapping herself in anger to shield herself from the pain. She'd had no time to wallow in tears and self-pity, or to give in to depression. One little boy had needed her. "About the other day. I never had a chance to really thank you." Only pure willpower kept her eyes from straying to the fine line of dark hair disappearing beneath the waistband of his jeans. "Petey loves that cat."

Her eyes looked dark, a deep blue green. A man might drown in them, Matt mused.

"It is supposed to be in the house, but it keeps sneaking out. In fact it was in the garage on the day of the fire."

Matt pivoted away and snatched his T-shirt from a tree branch. "It probably was looking for a corner somewhere to have its litter."

Surprise rushed in to her voice. "It's pregnant?"

"Couldn't you tell?"

"I never had a pet."

In one swift move, he tugged the shirt down over his head. Poor little rich girl. Matt doubted there was much else she'd done without. "Do you have more than him?"

"More than…?"

"Other children?"

She could barely manage the one she had. "No. I'm not married. Why did you ask?"

Matt lifted the bottom of the shirt to his face and wiped off sweat. "I wondered who else he had."

"Just me." Taylor glanced away, only looking back when the shirt again covered his flat, hard stomach. "Actually I have an aunt. So he has both of us."

"He told me he was playing hide-and-seek with Freddie."

"Freddie?" Taylor thought for a long moment. "Oh, the make-believe friend."

"You know, he's lonely," Matt said simply.

"Excuse me?" Thrown off balance by the unexpected and candid remark, she scowled at him. Did he think that she wasn't aware Petey was missing everything he'd lost?

In less time than it took to take a breath, a tinge of indignation had snapped into her voice. "Don't get in a huff," he said, not intending the words as criticism.

Taylor wanted to tell him, tell anyone who'd listen that she was doing the best she could. "I know he's lonely," she finally said, calming herself with what was obvious—that he wouldn't have brought the subject up if he hadn't been concerned about Petey.

For the boy's sake Matt was grateful she wasn't so self-absorbed that she was attuned to only herself.

"Aunt Taylor." Petey called loudly from where he stood in the kitchen doorway.

"I should leave." Mentally she grimaced. How inane that sounded. After all, he was a workman. That was why he was on her property. She didn't need to explain her actions to him. "Do you think you'll finish on schedule?"

Matt swung away and lifted a board from a pile of wood. Had she just delivered a subtle reminder that she was the one he worked for? He lined the board up with another one on his carpenter's sawhorse. "If it doesn't rain, I should."

Suddenly staring at his back, she realized *she'd* just been dismissed. As J. Harrington Elmhurst's daughter, she was usually treated well, even royally. Piqued, she whirled away to join Petey at the doorway.

"Matt's really great, isn't he, Aunt Taylor?" he questioned when she stepped near.

"Just great," she muttered, definitely not sure she even liked the man.

By seven that evening the sounds of hammering and sawing that had annoyed her all day had ended. Dressed in a sleeveless black sheath, she'd donned diamond-and-pearl earrings that had belonged to her mother and was waiting for other guests to come.

Sarah and her latest significant other, Brett Fornsworth II, had arrived first, and were cooing at each other near the buffet table.

Out the window Taylor saw a shiny gray limo and

moved to the foyer to greet her aunt. Madeline Elmhurst Crenshaw would never be considered sweet and adorable, but Taylor personally knew the caring warmth of her aunt.

In her early seventies, she was always well-groomed and expensively dressed. Though her figure had rounded, she looked exquisite in a gently flowing, black sequined dress, and her gray hair had recently been styled in a flattering, boyish cut.

When she stepped into the foyer, she brushed cheeks with Taylor, then pointed a well-manicured nail toward the opened door. "I was going to ask you how the boy is doing. But I saw him out in the yard with some man." She retraced her steps to the door. "Oh, my Lord."

Taylor noted that she looked as if she would faint.

"Come see what he's doing now. Your brother did not raise this child properly."

Taylor joined her to see Petey scooting on his knees through mud, and tunneling a truck through the muck. Even from a distance she could hear his "Zoom. Zoom."

Beside Petey, Matt was sitting back on his heels and laughing.

Her aunt rolled her eyes and turned away as Leeland reappeared from the vicinity of the kitchen. "Leeland, what is Peter doing?"

"I believe Master Peter said something about playing monster trucks."

"Ridiculous." She shook her head with disapproval, then gave a careless wave of her hand toward the door. "Leeland, bring him in, so he can get cleaned up."

Taylor mentally prepared herself for some well-meaning advice.

"This is what I'm talking about. Jared's provincial ideas have already taken hold. You may have gotten the boy just in time to straighten him out."

Taylor wondered if her aunt had any idea how lost she was about parenting. Taylor didn't know a thing about children.

From outside came the sound of a car engine. A woman's giggle announced the arrival of another guest. As the pear-shaped Vera, a distant cousin with an inclination for giggling, waddled up the walk, her aunt tapped her cane along the foyer's marble floor and made her way to the door to meet her. "By the way, Taylor, I'm absolutely certain that I've seen that man before."

Taylor said nothing. But hadn't she thought the same thing about Matt?

A night of too much champagne, too many hours with Vera's daughter, Kimmie, and her shrilly voice, and too much pressure from Ian about marriage made Taylor want to bury her head beneath a pillow the following morning.

The gesture was futile. A saw droned loudly. Then a hammer pounded. Groaning, she stretched beneath the sheet. Several moments passed before she lifted the eye mask to open one eye to the very early sunlight streaming in between the curtains. Certain there was no hope for more sleep, she eased from the bed.

She recalled how, during last night's party, a pediatrician had told her all kids liked to play arcade games. During breakfast she gave Petey a choice and wasn't surprised when he opted for the arcade instead of the movie. Just as they were leaving, she noticed that, after making all that noise early this morning, Matt had quit and left now that she was awake.

Sliding into the car beside Petey, she wondered if he had deliberately serenaded her at five this morning just to wake her up. She wouldn't doubt that one bit.

With directions from the pediatrician about where to go, Taylor drove them to the closest arcade at a strip mall in a neighboring town. It also had a store specializing in collectibles, including baseball cards. She remembered her brother mentioning Petey's interest in them.

Children, mostly boys, and a few adults filled the arcade. She and Petey waited their turn, then played air hockey. To his delight, she even sat beside him and pretended they were in an Indy car race. They spent another half hour in the nearby store while he chose baseball cards.

Excited, he shuffled the ones she'd purchased, examining each one over and over while they strolled toward the car. "Who's this?" he asked again and again.

Taylor read the card. "Ken Griffey."

"And this one?" At the slam of a truck door nearby, he looked away. "Aunt Taylor, look! There's Matt." He yelled out, "Matt! Matt!" Before she could stop him, he darted from her.

Under her breath Taylor muttered her displeasure,

but having no choice, she ambled in the same direction.

"And I got this one," Petey was saying when Taylor reached them. "He's Ken—Ken—" He paused and looked at Taylor for help as she drew near.

"Griffey," she told him.

"Griffey," Petey repeated. "We're going to have lunch. Matt could go, too. Couldn't you?"

"Where are you going?" he asked. Her jeans, sneakers and a yellow T-shirt made her appear more approachable today.

"I don't know," Petey said, and swung a questioning look up at Taylor.

Matt guessed that meant she hadn't asked the boy and probably planned on lobster bisque at some swanky hotel.

Taylor had intended to take Petey to a nearby resort with its sweeping view of the desert. "It's Petey's choice today," she said, because she felt guilty that she hadn't thought to find out where he would like to go.

"Mr. Hamburger. Mr. Hamburger," Petey shouted.

Taylor struggled to veil her distress. Mr. Hamburger meant greasy burgers and French fries.

"My favorite place," Matt responded. Joining them for lunch had never crossed his mind until he'd seen the agony that had popped into her eyes over Petey's selection. He had to witness the lady of the manor dipping fat-drenched fries in a puddle of mustard.

"Petey, there might not be one nearby," Taylor said, hoping she was right.

"Sure there is. It's around here somewhere. Daddy always took me when we came to see you."

Taylor saw the sadness flicker in his eyes.

Matt did, too. "I know where it is. It's next to the batting cages. Ever been there?" he asked to distract him.

"I'm too little," he answered.

"You won't always be," Taylor said encouragingly. "Then we'll go there. Why don't you lead to Mr. Hamburger," she suggested to Matt.

"Follow my chariot," Matt said.

Petey turned puzzled eyes up at Taylor.

"He means his truck," she said lightly.

"Oh." He gave her the grin she and Matt had been working for.

For a few minutes they'd joined forces to not let Petey's sadness grab hold. And for those few minutes, she'd really liked him. In all honesty, she had to admit that he'd done nothing but try to help Petey.

On top of that thought came another. As she followed his white truck into the parking lot of Mr. Hamburger, an idea, unexpected and downright disturbing, flashed across her mind. She frowned, not sure she liked it, and decided she needed to give it a lot more thought.

She'd surprised him, Matt realized, as he carried their tray of food to a booth in the fast-food restaurant. She'd revealed a softness, a sensitivity he hadn't expected, when she'd tried to keep the boy from dwelling on the loss of his father. She also bore up amazingly well to what she might view as an unpleasant experience, not even grimacing when he set a tray before her that was ladened with cups of soda, French fries, her salad, his hamburger, and breaded chicken pieces for Petey.

This was a definite first, Taylor mused. She doubted any Elmhurst other than her brother had ever set a foot in one of these restaurants. She took in the colorful molded plastic tables and benches and the ball pit and slide play area, then settled beside Petey on a bright aqua bench. "Here." She placed a small white bag of French fries and one of chicken in front of him.

"This is better than them dumb old Brussels sprouts." He wrinkled his nose with disgust.

Matt bit into his hamburger and chuckled. "Who gave you Brussels sprouts?"

Since she would be named soon, Taylor confessed. "They're good for you."

Matt couldn't help smiling. It was something a mother would say. "I like corn on the cob."

"Me, too," Petey said enthusiastically while he dipped his breaded chicken piece into the ketchup. He flashed Matt another one of his irresistible grins. "And I like French fries."

Matt played the game. "Me, too."

Taylor poked a fork in to her salad. She felt as if she were the only adult present.

The steady stream of conversation came from Petey. That seemed best. Taylor couldn't imagine having anything in common with the man sitting across the table from her. "Aunt Taylor has a computer," Petey told him.

Matt noted the faint dimple cutting into her right cheek. "Do you play games on it?"

His mouth full, Petey bobbed his head.

Though Matt used his computer for his business, he'd spent his share of time playing games on it. "What kind of games?" he asked as he thought of the sports software he'd collected.

"There's a game about this car that goes to the moon and can't get back without finding some things—like a lunchbox and a flashlight. And there's another one about a fish trying to catch a ghost. And there's some mean sharks."

"Do you like to fish?"

"I never went." The light suddenly dimmed in his eyes. "My daddy was going to take me."

Mentally Matt cursed. The last thing he'd meant to do was revive the boy's heartache. "I have a game for the computer that lets you catch fish."

"Real fishing?" he asked with some interest.

"Just like it. I'll bring it with me tomorrow and you can play it on the computer."

"Okay," Petey answered distractedly when three boys and a girl about his age dashed toward the slide. "Can I go, Aunt Taylor?"

Taylor hesitated. Was it safe? Would other parents let their children play there if it wasn't? "Yes." He was already standing, gulping a swallow of his drink. "But we can't stay too long," she added. She barely got out the last word, and he was gone.

Shoes off, he dived into the area filled with balls. For a long moment, mainly to avoid the gray eyes on her, she watched Petey scampering behind other kids and into a long and colorful, molded-plastic tunnel. Men rarely made her nervous. The man sitting across the table from her definitely did.

Matt wiped his hands on the napkin and balled it. She was out of his class. But that didn't mean he wasn't interested. She was soft, more aware of others than he'd expected, lacking the hard edge Alisha'd had. And he found her as attractive now as he had five years ago. "We met before, you know. At a charity function."

Taylor looked up, puzzled. She'd thought he looked familiar. "Where?"

"The ballroom of the Crystal Hotel."

She recalled that she'd been bored silly that evening. Her companion had been the grandson of a corporate bigwig, one her aunt had clearly been impressed with. He'd droned on about his latest successful acquisition for his company. She had nodded, and smiled at all the right moments and had vowed to finish out the evening, but to never endure another one with him. Her eyes narrowing, she stared hard at Matt. It took only a minute. With a place and time to trigger the memory, she remembered him now.

Weary of her date's company, she'd stepped outside for a moment and had seen a dark-haired, handsome man standing in the shadows near a rose trellis. Wearing a dark tuxedo, he'd looked as tired as she'd felt that night. He'd turned, his eyes had met hers. There had been a softer look to them then, and a smile. A second later, her date had found her. "Were you a donator?" she asked, her curiosity aroused as she wondered how a carpenter had afforded a pricey dinner at a charity function.

Matt viewed himself as a jeans and T-shirt man. He loved pot roast and mashed potatoes, not stuff with French names. He enjoyed action-adventure movies, not foreign films. At heart, he was a small-town Ohio boy. "Having trouble believing I belonged there?"

"I'm not a snob, Mr. Duran." Irritation came quickly, though Taylor was honest enough with herself to recognize that she was being thin-skinned because he'd gotten so close to the truth. Looking down, she gathered the napkins and greasy wrappers.

"That wasn't meant as an insult," Matt was quick to say. He closed a hand over hers, stilling it.

Unexpectedly a jolt whipped through Taylor. She jerked, unprepared for the sensation or the reaction. Within a second, he freed her hand. But it was a second too late. Her heart was beating a touch faster, her blood had heated. She realized he was saying something about a baseball game and Petey, but it took another second for her to gather her wits. "You want to take him to a baseball game?"

"A baseball game?" Petey asked excitedly, suddenly standing beside them.

Taylor wished he hadn't overheard until she'd had time to think about the invitation from a man who was still a stranger.

"Can we go?" Petey caught her hesitation.

Desperately Taylor wanted her relationship with Petey to deepen. She loved the sweet boy who hugged and kissed her as if they'd always been together. But the notion of spending a day with this man made her uneasy.

"Can we go?" Petey asked again.

"You can let me know," Matt said, taking the pressure off her to give him an answer right now.

"I will." She touched Petey's shoulder. "We need to leave."

Matt visually followed them out the door. He doubted that she would go. She was the type who attended polo games; she'd probably never even been to a baseball game. And he shouldn't want to spend more time with her. He downed the last of his soda. Already he knew that his blood stirred when she was near.

Chapter Three

Three days had passed since their lunch. Taylor had avoided seeing Matt but hadn't been able to stop thinking about him, about the way his touch had fluttered her heart as if she were sixteen again. And Petey wouldn't let her forget about the invitation to the baseball game. At least ten times a day, he'd asked her about it. She'd been too cowardly to tell him outright that they weren't going. Then last night that idea, the one she wasn't entirely sure she liked, had popped into her brain again.

She'd been sitting on the terrace at dusk, enjoying an iced tea, and had noticed a pile of lumber near her petunia garden. "What's that?" she'd asked Leeland when he'd returned with the iced tea pitcher.

"I believe Master Peter said it's going to be a fort.

He and Matt—Mr. Duran,'' he corrected, ''started building it several days ago.''

At that moment her idea no longer seemed so ludicrous, and she realized Matt Duran might provide a solution to her problem with Petey.

The morning rain had canceled her golf game, and though she usually spent such days shopping, she backed off from Sarah's suggestion that they hop in her cousin's Cessna and fly to California.

She had more important things to deal with.

Swirling his spoon in the cereal bowl, Petey didn't greet her when she sat at the table across from him. It took a game of twenty questions before Taylor pulled the reason out of him.

''You never signed the note for the trip to the museum.''

Taylor racked her brain, trying to remember where she'd set the note.

''It's for today. I can't go.'' Blue eyes filled with accusations drilled her from across the wide, highly polished dining room table.

''Of course, you can.''

''No, I can't.'' The threat of tears tightened his voice.

''Yes, you can.'' Taylor didn't understand why he was making so much of it. ''I'll get the note,'' she said simply. ''I'll sign it.''

''It's too late.''

He was overreacting, she decided. It couldn't be too late.

''Ms. Fremp said we couldn't go if we didn't bring the permission slip in on time.''

Her stomach knotted with tension. She couldn't let this happen.

"I was supposed to bring the note in yesterday."

"I'll go to school with you." Taylor pushed back her chair. "I'll talk to your teacher." She said the last word while rushing out of the room.

Taylor found the note she'd transferred from her purse to a desk drawer, signed it, dressed quickly and drove Petey to school. His teacher wasn't the most understanding. Rules were rules, she'd said when Taylor tried to hand her the signed permission slip. Yesterday was the deadline.

Taylor didn't give a hoot about deadlines. One little boy's feelings mattered most. Why should he be punished because she'd forgotten to sign the note? He'd even mentioned it to her at breakfast two days ago. This was her fault, not his. After all he'd been through, she couldn't let him down.

Taylor saw the director's name on a sheet of stationery on the woman's desk and bluffed. "Perhaps I could talk to Mr. Bowman. George and I might be able to work this out," Taylor said, as if they were old friends.

The woman's face flushed. "Well—I suppose this once I could make an exception."

Taylor said a silent prayer of thanks that the woman had acquiesced. The bluff had worked, but more important Petey hugged her before she left him. She was relieved that everything had worked out.

Driving home, she felt emotionally exhausted. She'd worked endless hours for charities and had never felt quite so drained. All because of a permission slip.

In the living room she flopped on the sofa. Slowly she sipped her first cup of tea and relaxed to the soft, lulling strains of Beethoven's concerto in B flat minor.

Staring out the window, she watched rain plop on the water in the swimming pool. She could wait until tomorrow or the next day when Matt was working again to talk to him, but impatience nagged at her. For Petey's sake, she couldn't afford to wait too long. "Leeland, do you have Mr. Duran's business card?"

"Yes, miss."

Since he wasn't coming today, she would go to him.

"You'll be going out, miss?"

She fingered the business card Leeland had handed her. "Yes."

"Do you want John," he asked about her chauffeur, "to bring the car around?"

"No. I'll drive myself."

Windshield wipers swished at the rain streaming down the window. With the business card in her hand, Taylor realized now that Matt's business was in the same strip mall she'd gone to with Petey. Far north of Phoenix, the town had a rustic Western appearance. Though expensive, adobe-style homes dotted the bottom of the mountain, around the main streets, stores promoted the authentic Western look to attract the tourists that the town counted on.

How quaint, her mother would have said. It occurred to Taylor that her mother would view this trip to see Matt as inappropriate, beneath an Elmhurst. Though her mother had been dead nine years, Taylor could still recall the edginess that had always crept into her mother's voice when she'd reprimanded her.

"You should have summoned him," she'd have said.

Because, of course, an Elmhurst didn't step down to the common level. But her mother had been wrong. An Elmhurst had left to do just that. And her brother had never seemed to regret it.

Taylor parked at the curb in front of a shop with a sign that simply stated "Duran's." She'd expected a small office; instead, a large warehouse building housed his business. She switched off the ignition, then reached under her seat for her umbrella. Through the rain, she dashed from her car to his shop.

A "Gone to Lunch" sign hung in the window of the door, blocking her view of the inside of the shop. Muttering a curse, she scanned the stores along the street and spotted a diner at the corner. She had nothing to lose, she decided, and sprinted beneath the store overhangs to the diner.

As she opened the door, a bell above it jingled. Inside, red vinyl booths lined a window wall. Matching stools bordered the counter. Behind it, a gaunt man flipped a hamburger patty and a woman with ample hips and brassy blond hair flashed a smile of crooked teeth at a customer while she poured coffee in his cup. Standing near the antiquated cash register stood a man with hair so neatly combed it looked like a silver helmet.

Taylor stayed at the door until she located Matt at a table by the windows. She realized he'd probably seen her before she'd entered. With his back against the wall, and his long, denim-clad legs stretched out beneath the table, he smiled slowly. Just as slowly his eyes moved over her. Taylor fought a swell of uneasiness while she crossed the pine floor. She wasn't here on some whim or impulsive act. She had a rehearsed speech. She had a goal. She needed this man and his friendship. So as she neared his table, she forced a smile, despite feeling awkward and uncertain. "May I sit down?"

The last person Matt had expected to see strolling in to Ernie's Diner was her. Manners finally kicking in, he stood. He noticed one of the good-old boys sitting on a stool at the counter nearly fell off it to see her. "I'm sorry." He laughed at himself. "I never expected to see you here." Dressed in cream-colored slacks and a matching, long-sleeved blouse, she looked tailored, classy, out of place.

"How did you find me?" he asked once she'd taken a seat.

"This place was the closest to your shop. The sign on your door reminded me of a scene from one of those old movies where the doctor leaves a 'Gone Fishing' sign on the door," she said, the smile still plastered to her face to keep her own tension at bay.

"Sounds like a James Stewart movie." In fascination, he noticed the way the overhead lights highlighted the sun-bleached strands in her blond hair.

Setting her purse on the seat beside her, Taylor

worked at relaxing and took one long, deep breath. "Do you like old movies?"

"Doesn't everyone?" There was something sweet about her. The thought flashed through his mind with no warning. God, maybe he was losing all objectivity? He didn't know her. After being fooled by one woman, he should have been more wary. She'd come looking for him. *Why* was the big question.

"I thought you would just have an office somewhere. Construction is on-site work. Why have the big building?"

"I refinish furniture, too."

"Oh, I didn't know."

Matt nearly smiled. She looked so serious. "Who recommended me for the job of rebuilding your garage?" he asked, while nodding at someone passing by.

"A friend of my lawyer's." The man had raved that Matt Duran was a superb craftsman. She thought it odd that someone so highly regarded had nothing more than a one-man business, then she'd learned he'd had a successful business and had lost it. "Are you from here?" she asked, grateful he wasn't pressuring her for a reason why she'd come looking for him. After all, she could hardly just blurt out what she needed from him.

Matt sipped his coffee. What was this all about? "Ohio." He smiled at an elderly woman who'd paused outside the window to wave at him. Edna Fenten had been one of his first customers when he'd arrived in town.

Taylor realized he was well liked, respected. She'd

taken a chance coming to him. She didn't know him, but she considered herself good at judging people. Now she only had one more question to ask before she shared her idea with him. "Are you married?" She'd already noted that he wore no wedding band.

For the second time in minutes, she knocked him off balance. "Am I—"

"Married." It might matter if he was single or married.

Matt had thought he would be married by now. There had been a time when he'd believed his life wouldn't be complete without a wife and a family. But marriage, the kind his parents had, the kind that lasted, required trust. He wasn't sure he could give that to any woman ever again.

"No, I'm not," he said with a mixture of wariness and amusement as he wondered where the conversation was headed.

"Good." Now was as good a time as any, she mused. "I'd like to talk to you about Petey."

Matt frowned, totally puzzled. Why did it matter if he was married? And what did she want to say about the boy? He watched her hands, the slender fingers linking so tightly that her knuckles whitened.

"Petey's adjusted well to the tragedy of losing his parents. But you were right. He is lonely." Nervously she smoothed the napkin on her lap. "He doesn't have the friends he had at the apartment building, someone to play ball with. He's used to a different life-style," she explained. "He told you that I bought him a computer and software games. He plays with them, but sometimes he looks so bored."

Matt liked the kid, had felt the boy reaching out to him. He didn't doubt the aunt was doing all she could. It was clear to Matt that she loved the boy, but he needed all the affection he could get right now.

"My life is so different for him."

"Why is it? He's your brother's son, isn't he?" Matt saw a frown shadowing her eyes. "Didn't he have money, too?"

His probing stare insisted she be totally honest with him. "My brother thumbed his nose at the family money."

Matt doubted she'd planned to air family problems. But she started this, not him. "Why did he?"

Taylor made herself go on. "Because of Elizabeth, my sister-in-law. Years ago, determined to be his own person, Jared gave up everything for her."

Matt asked the obvious question. "Who made him do that?"

He was perceptive. "My father never approved of Elizabeth."

Matt had a good idea what reason her family had come up with, but he asked, "Why not?"

Would he understand she wasn't like her father? She hoped so. "Elizabeth·was a sales clerk when Jared met her. My father expected my brother to marry someone more suitable."

Matt said nothing. What she meant was clear. Her father had viewed the woman as too common. Responding to the click of heels, Matt raised his gaze from her to the diner's only waitress.

In her tight pink uniform with her hair piled atop her head, Shirley lifted her order pad in the air and pulled a pen from its tucked position behind her ear. "So what are you folks going to have?"

"Coffee," Taylor said, but her stomach rumbled, reminding her that she hadn't eaten. She flipped open the plastic-coated menu. The daily special was Roundup Stew. "I'll have coffee and a bacon, lettuce and tomato sandwich."

Matt waited until Shirley looked at him. "How's the roast—" As Shirley wrinkled her nose, he stopped.

"Order the pork tenderloin sandwich," she suggested.

His eyes met and held Shirley's as he spoke. "If you say so."

"Right-o, Matt."

Taylor could again see he was well liked. He'd given his full attention to Shirley, made her feel important. Perhaps Petey had felt all of that too when he was with Matt.

"Go on with your story."

Tiredness suddenly swept over her at having to share so much with a stranger. A pounding began at the base of her skull. "My brother and father argued."

Reliving that memory wasn't easy. She recalled crying, standing in the hallway, listening to them. Jared had offered her the only security she'd known. "He left then," she said simply. She'd been twelve and suddenly on her own, because Jared had refused to knuckle under and stop seeing Elizabeth. As a child, hurting, she'd wondered how he could turn his back on what he'd always had, on the people who cared about him—on her. She'd loved him, she'd missed him, she'd yearned for her brother's company, and he'd walked away. "He gave up a lot to be with Elizabeth." She grew quiet as Shirley stopped beside the table to set down her coffee cup.

Matt had been raised by people who'd been a couple for over thirty years. Sometimes his parents had struggled financially. He remembered one spring when it rained intermittently for two weeks and brought construction work to a standstill. Money had been tight, and his dad had gone to work at a factory on the nightshift to support his family. He'd come home at three in the morning, and Matt's mom would always be awake, waiting for her husband. What they'd been without hadn't been as important as what they'd had—each other.

"My brother chose to live a middle-class life with his wife and their son," Taylor said when the waitress moved away. She recalled occasional visits to her brother's home that first year. He and Elizabeth had seemed so happy. Then her father had stopped letting her visit them. She'd had no contact with them until after her twenty-first birthday. She'd been a part of their celebration when, after ten years together, Elizabeth had become pregnant.

With her silence, Matt had time to think. It dawned on him what her problem was. The boy wasn't used to his aunt's privileged life-style.

Taylor said as much. "Petey's had a life of baseball games, barbecues, playing in the park. Everything is so different for him with me." Gently she rubbed at a shoulder tight with tension. "I think he misses that life as much as he does his parents." Too much was at stake for Taylor not to be candid. "I—I don't know how to be a parent. This is all so new to me."

Matt poured cream into his coffee. What did she want from him? He wasn't a parent. "Why are you telling me all this?"

"My associations are with people who—" Taylor paused. What she'd been about to say might sound insulting. "I don't know anyone who's familiar with the way of life he's used to."

Staring at the steaming brew in his cup, Matt reached for a spoon. What she wanted was clear. She needed a common man's touch in Petey's life, and she'd picked him. "What you mean is you don't know anyone who isn't rich."

Taylor mentally grimaced. He was going to make her sound like a snob. "Please, I need help." She hated the admittance. "I need instructions, directions, something. I need to offer Petey what he's used to."

Aware of Shirley's nosiness when she came to slide plates of food on the table, Matt temporarily halted the conversation. "Looks good, Shirl." Whatever Taylor had to say to him was her business, not the whole diner's.

Shirley cracked her gum. "Told you."

Taylor waited until the waitress stepped away. "I hope you understand. I can give Petey everything Jared couldn't. Petey will have an exemplary education."

Oh, hell. What did that mean? Boarding school? Matt stifled his annoyance.

Taylor watched him dab a French fry in a puddle

of ketchup. Did he understand? "From what Petey has said, he and my brother played catch." Taylor took a bite of her sandwich. The food was better than she'd expected, the lettuce crisp, the tomato juicy. Shirley refilled Matt's coffee cup then slapped a check on the table near Matt's cup. "I don't know how to do that," Taylor admitted when they were alone again.

Matt sent her a look of disbelief. "Come on. Everyone knows how to catch a ball."

"Not with one of those gloves," Taylor said in her defense. She'd put it on her hand and wondered how anyone caught a ball with one of them.

A trace of humor tugged at the corners of his lips. "Do you play any sport?"

"Tennis. And eventually I'll see that Petey learns how to play polo."

Matt salted the meat on his sandwich, then took a bite. Since he'd never been on a horse, he didn't doubt that he would break his neck if he tried to play polo.

"Leeland's been helping, but he's unable to give Petey what he needs." Vividly she recalled her butler's pained expression when he'd chased after the balls Petey had thrown at him. "So I purchased a batting machine and one of those nets where, I guess, you throw the ball at the net, and the ball bounces back. Petey played with the machine once, but hasn't since."

Matt viewed her over the rim of his coffee cup. She really knew nothing about kids, he decided. "And you don't know why."

"I thought he would like it." Unable to eat, she set down the sandwich half. "He loves baseball."

His gaze didn't waver from hers. "So you figured a batting machine would make him happy."

She was certain she heard criticism in his voice, but she couldn't afford to get touchy now. "I realize he needs someone to work with him." She geared up her courage. "That's why I came to you. He obviously likes you. Would you help?" She drew a deep, calming breath, prayed he didn't laugh in her face now that she'd told him. "I realize it's a lot to ask of you. That's why I'd wondered if you were married. I doubt a wife would be thrilled to have you give up time to spend with him."

At first Matt hadn't taken her seriously. But clearly she'd thought out her plan.

"Of course, I'm willing to pay."

Matt stopped chewing and frowned at her. "Pay for what?"

"Whatever you want to call it. His father is gone. He needs male companionship."

"A hired father?" Matt asked.

"Yes, I suppose so."

Matt pinched a French fry from his plate. He didn't need to be hired. He'd sensed the boy's need for male company. Whenever he'd had free time while on the job, he'd spent it with him. It wasn't a hardship. The boy was polite, inquisitive, fun to talk to. And Matt had enjoyed the few times they'd played ball.

"I know it will take longer for you to finish my garage. That's all right." If her garage never got built, she could care less. Petey was all that mattered to her. "I'll make it worthwhile."

She just confirmed what he'd learned years ago. Moneyed people thought the almighty buck could handle anything. What jerk would take money to play ball with a kid?

"Will you think about it?" She stood to leave and reached into her shoulder bag for her wallet.

"I've got it," Matt insisted.

Taylor didn't argue. He looked like a man with an enormous amount of pride. Dropping her wallet back in her purse, she remembered what else she wanted to say. "About the baseball game—"

Matt made a logical assumption. Since she planned to pay him for his time with the boy, he assumed she would let Petey go with him.

Sliding the strap of her purse to her shoulder, she told him, "We'd both like to go."

Both? "Both of you?"

She wanted to be a part of a day she knew would be special to Petey. "Yes. Is that all right?" In a small show of nerves, she gripped the purse strap tighter.

"Sure." She kept throwing him off balance, he realized, as he visually followed her to the door. Why the hell wasn't she fitting neatly into the slot? Puzzled, he stared at the dark brew in his cup.

"You're scowling."

Blinking, he found himself face-to-face with his sister. "I didn't know you were here."

"Ditto. I was in back talking to Louise. She brought her granddaughter in. She's so cute. Forget that,'' she said, seeming alert to her rambling. "Shirley told me you had female company. I missed seeing her." She was smiling now. "Who was she?" His sister had many smiles. This was her speculative one.

"Taylor Elmhurst."

In a heartbeat, a frown replaced her smile. "What was she doing here?" Like a blind person, she felt behind her for a chair, then sat.

"She was talking to me about a job." His sister didn't need to know everything.

"I remember Alisha seemed interested in where you lived and—"

Spoiled and bored, Alisha had been looking for a diversion and had chosen him. "She isn't Alisha," he reminded her. Taylor was different than he'd expected, genuinely caring about the boy. And he liked talking to her.

Maybe that was the real problem, he mused. More than once he'd dropped his guard with her.

Rain stopped at four that afternoon, only to resume at midnight. Matt awoke to the sound of thunder, and gave up trying to get back to sleep. Even an hour of watching a documentary about sharks on TV failed to make him sleepy.

Wide awake at 5:00 a.m., he roused himself and collected dirty laundry. Short one sock, he hunted for it. In a likely spot, under the bed, he found instead a paperback he'd started reading in bed last week, while the missing sock hid behind the dresser.

Before seven he finished the laundry, including folding and putting everything away. Showered and shaved, he dressed slowly, distracted by thoughts. He was honest enough with himself to admit that his restlessness had more to do with a certain slim blonde than with the rain.

Crazy thinking, he berated himself. Any involvement with her was because of the boy. For his own peace of mind, he didn't need to keep thinking about that curving mouth or imagining how she would feel beneath his hands.

All he needed was to get busy. The feel of wood beneath his hands was a guarantee to lift his gloomy mood. He derived pleasure from simple things—a hammer in his hand, cheese pizza, a walk at sunrise, the sight of the orange morning sky.

But instead of heading toward his shop, he strolled into the room that he'd equipped like a gym. Was this all about lust? he wondered. How could it be? He'd never even kissed her. Hell, she might kiss like a wet fish.

He laughed at that thought. If he was any judge of women, which he used to think he was, she would deliver a kiss that would knock him on his backside.

Matt slid two forty-five-pound weights on each side of the bar. Some heavy-duty exercise might get her image out of his mind.

In minutes perspiration soaked his clothes. No matter how often he worked out with weights, his muscles still protested. Grunting, he pressed the bar up again.

He had friends he could call and spend an enjoyable dinner with. He never wanted for company. So why in the hell was he feeling so annoyed that it was raining, that he wouldn't see her?

At the ring of the phone, he set down the free weights and sat up from the bench press. He let the answering machine take the call while he snatched a towel off the end of the rack. It was the sound of Petey's youthful voice that made him reach for the receiver.

Chapter Four

"Petey?"

"Hi, Matt. Is it okay that I called?"

"Yeah." He could see the kid's eager smile. "How did you find my phone number?"

"It was on that little card."

Matt assumed he meant his business card. He wiped his face with the towel while he wandered into the kitchen. "What's going on, champ?"

"Remember you said I could see the train you have."

Matt poured himself a cup of coffee as he recalled the brief one minute conversation with Petey about the model train.

"Could I see it today? I don't have any school. The teachers have a meeting."

"Free day, huh?"

"Yeah, so could I?"

Matt took a quick swallow of coffee, then opened a cupboard and hunted for something to eat. "Does your aunt know you're calling me?"

"She wouldn't care."

Matt guessed the answer was no, which meant she hadn't told Petey to call him. He stuck his hand into a box of opened cereal. "I tell you what we'll do. You go talk to your aunt." Before he'd left the diner that day, he'd made a decision to spend time with the boy. "If she says it's okay, I'll come get you."

"Okay, Matt."

He was suddenly left holding a silent phone. Amused, he put down the receiver and tossed the cereal into his mouth. Definitely stale. Ceremoniously he dropped the box of cereal in the garbage can, then picked up the receiver again. Just in time, it seemed.

"She said she'll call you," Petey said breathlessly as if he'd been running. Without a goodbye, he hung up.

Matt laughed and set down the receiver, his mind already on what to buy at the store for his breakfast. He made a quick run across the street to the convenience market.

When he returned, the first thing he did was check the answering machine. She hadn't called him. Hell, she might have said that to appease the boy. Don't play a fool. Not again, he warned himself.

Straddling a kitchen chair, he pondered the newspaper crossword puzzle while he finished a miniature, powdered sugar doughnut and a second cup of coffee.

Twenty minutes later, he glared at the telephone

with some annoyance as it rang again. It was the third call since he'd gotten back from the store. None of the calls had been from her. The first solicitor wanted to give him a free weekend in Las Vegas. The second one offered a new long-distance phone service. He figured this call was from some charitable institute asking for thrift shop donations. A no on the tip of his tongue, he picked up the phone.

Taylor's soft smoky-sounding hello kept him silent.

"Petey said you invited him over to see a model train."

Matt grinned. It occurred to him that the kid might be manipulating them. "That's right."

"I was going to take him to the amusement park today, but it's raining. We'd like to come."

We. That was interesting. "Okay." He shot a look at the wall clock. "I'll pick you up. Probably eleven-thirty."

"I can drive there."

He thought about the roads outside of town. "If it keeps raining, you'll be better in a truck."

"Matt? Does this mean you're taking the job?"

"It's not a job."

"I—"

"No money," Matt insisted.

"Yes, all right."

He heard her goodbye, but what was more important, he heard the smile in her voice.

Though prone to arriving late, he entered the kitchen of her house at 11:20. He'd liked the kitchen the first time he'd entered it. Blue and white with copper pans hanging from rafters, it was homey, comfortable and almost always smelled of freshly baked goods.

In the middle of the room, Lottie rolled dough on a trestle table. With the door closing behind him, she raised her head and greeted him with a smile. "I didn't expect to see you today." She stopped, wiped her hands on a towel and pivoted away to pour him a cup of coffee. "With it raining, you can't work, can you?"

Matt wiped a hand across his damp face. "I'm here to pick up Petey."

"Miss Taylor asked that you meet them in the living room," Leeland said from the doorway.

Confusion etched into Lottie's face. "I thought her aunt was visiting."

"I believe she's leaving," Leeland answered. "If you'd follow me, sir."

The sir reference stopped Matt in midstep. Apparently his status had changed in the man's eyes, because Matt was going to spend time with the mistress of the house. Before everything got out of hand, Matt touched Leeland's shoulder to get his attention. During the past weeks, along with coffee and lunches in the kitchen, Matt had gotten familiar with Leeland and Lottie and learned they'd been employed in the Elmhurst household since before Taylor was born. "Don't get weird on me, Leeland. You know my name. It's not sir," he said, sweeping a glance at Lottie so she'd know that was meant for her, too.

Leeland looked unconvinced. "Yes, but—"

"No buts." Matt walked beside him down the hall. "I'm no different today than yesterday," he assured him before they reached the living room. It was large and contained several beige sofas and chairs near a grand piano. Two others in a lighter shade were located near a brick fireplace. Matt scanned the paintings, mostly watercolors, set in elaborate gold frames. The furnishings were classic, tasteful and similar to another house. *You've been here before,* he reminded himself, thinking back to Alisha's home. If he had any sense, he wouldn't stay.

At the other end of the house, Taylor opened the door of the study for her aunt. Seconds ago she'd frozen in place on the way to the door and had looked at Taylor as if she'd announced she was getting her nose pierced. "Where did you say you're going?"

"To his home." Taylor already sensed she'd made a giant mistake mentioning Matt had invited Petey and her this afternoon. "I asked him to help with Petey."

Her aunt's gray brows bunched in a frown. "Why in the world would you do that?"

"Because I need help." There she'd said it aloud. "Petey's lived—"

"Like a commoner," her aunt interrupted.

Oh, don't make this difficult for me, she wanted to beg. *I'm doing as best I can.* "Petey likes being around him."

Some of Taylor's uneasiness must have come through. An understanding look came to her aunt's face. And rather than criticism, concern laced her tone. "Are you paying this man?"

"I offered but he refused."

Her aunt's pale blue eyes narrowed. "Why would he do this for nothing?"

Taylor turned a frown on her. "What?"

"Why would he? Why would he care about someone else's little boy?"

Again Taylor wished they'd never started this discussion. She didn't want to doubt his motives. What about kindness? she wanted to say. Maybe he saw a little boy needing him and had simply reached out to Petey. Why couldn't Matt Duran be a nice man?

"A woman of wealth must always be cautious in such matters, Taylor. Money, darling," she said for emphasis while they strolled down the hallway to the front door, "is why he's so agreeable."

Taylor wanted to disagree.

"What other reason could he have for showing such an interest?"

Taylor thought it was obvious. "Petey's a wonderful little boy."

"And you, my darling," she said, facing Taylor and brushing a gentle finger across her cheek, "you're beautiful and charming, quite appealing. But you can not afford to accept this man at face value. This can be quite dangerous and expensive for you if you're not careful."

Taylor chose the path of least resistance and said nothing. This, whatever *this* was, wasn't about her and Matt. They were together because of Petey. But her aunt's advice came for a good reason. There had been another man who'd done just that to her. Justin Barrett had made her nineteen-year-old pulse skip. He'd also hurt her badly enough to teach her a lesson she would never forget. But that was a decade ago. She wasn't quite so gullible anymore.

"Call me tomorrow," her aunt requested before stepping outside toward her limo.

As Taylor closed the door, she heard the sound of Petey's voice from the other room, indicating he'd already joined Matt.

Earlier, when she'd opened her eyes to the dreary morning and the rain, she'd thought she would be pulling out her hair to think of things to keep Petey occupied. Then Petey had told her that Matt had called. She was really grateful he'd accepted the plan she'd suggested.

Strolling toward the two of them, she smiled at the sight of their heads bent close together while Petey showed Matt his prize possession, an album of baseball cards he'd collected.

"I'll show you the ones I have when we get to my place," Matt told him. He was already thinking about several cards that the boy would value. Looking up, he saw Taylor watching them. A smile curled her lips. She was dressed in jeans and a pale blue, loose-fitting blouse over a white, scoop-necked T-shirt. With her hair tucked behind her ears, she looked young and more like a college coed than one of society's most influential women. "Ready?"

"Yes." Though his eyes locked with hers for only a second, her mouth went suddenly dry. And in that instant she knew her aunt might be right. Both of them wanted to help Petey, but everything that was happening between them wasn't only about him.

"Let's go, champ." Matt didn't need her to say

more. He saw nervousness in her eyes, in the way she stood with finishing-school straightness. "Meet you at the truck."

Petey's face brightened with a smile. "We're going in the truck?"

"In the truck." Matt had anticipated that the boy would really like it. He'd noticed Taylor had Petey driven to school in the limo, and imagined the impression that made on classmates. While girls in Petey's class might think the limo was really neat or whatever term they used today for something good, boys would taunt him about it for no reason except that the limo made Petey different from them and gave them something to tease him about.

"Cool! That's bad, isn't it, Aunt Taylor?"

"Bad," she mumbled, aware that meant just the opposite.

Inside his truck Matt squinted through the rain-splattered window as slanting drops curtained the view and thundered on the roof. "Did you ever learn how the fire started?" he asked, looking for conversation.

Taylor was grateful that Petey sat between them. She couldn't recall feeling so unnerved with a male since she was fifteen. "The fire department told me there was a frayed wire in a socket."

"The fire engine was really big," Petey piped in.

Matt grinned at him before he zipped into an alley behind stores. When he was a kid, he'd been just as delighted over a trip with his dad to the local fire department.

Taylor hadn't paid enormous attention to where they were until minutes ago. Now confusion settled over her as she viewed her surroundings. Matt had driven to his shop. "Why are we here?"

"I live here. I have an apartment behind my shop."

Her mother's voice surfaced in her brain. *He's unsuitable, Taylor.*

"Wow," Petey said as thunder rumbled with earthshaking strength over them.

Holding on to Petey, Taylor stepped out of the truck to the rush of wind and pelting rain.

"It's this way," Matt yelled over the howl of the wind as he came around the front of the truck.

Overjoyed with the rain, Petey stood with arms outstretched, head back, tongue out and tried to catch raindrops.

Without a falter in his stride, Matt touched the small of Taylor's back to nudge her forward and caught Petey under his other arm. "Come on, champ."

His face glowing, Petey giggled at the jostling sideways ride in the cradle of Matt's arm. Smiling, Taylor ran with them. Wasn't all this about hearing the sound of Petey's laughter, about easing away some of the sadness he felt?

When they reached the steel door, she followed them in to what Matt called home, a building that resembled a garage-size warehouse. Sparsely decorated, the room in front of her contained barbells and a bench press. Standing beside her, Petey's eyes grew wide when he spotted the set of gymnast's rings dangling from the ceiling.

A hand on his shoulder, Taylor urged him to follow. They walked through a white-and-black kitchen that was so small they had to go single file through it to the next room. In a far corner, a round oak table was near a window, along with a ficus plant and a wicker trunk. She crossed the shiny planked floor, and decided instantly that he cluttered. Books occupied the top of an ottoman, newspapers were stacked near one of the cushiony-looking hunter green chairs, cellophane candy wrappers were balled on a tabletop. Though basically clean, he obviously didn't pick up daily.

"Here's the train," he was saying to Petey.

Set up on a coffee table was a miniature train and village.

Petey's eyes widened. "It's so small."

In passing, Matt handed Taylor a towel to dry off. "It's the smallest train you can get. N-gauge," he told him. "It was my dad's."

While Petey oohed about the train, Taylor ran the towel over her damp arms and wandered to the photographs displayed on an end table. In one of them, a bright-eyed youngster of about nine with a toothless grin proudly showed off a baseball trophy.

"My cousin Jeff's son," Matt said about the framed photograph she'd picked up. "They live in Ohio. I've got wine—"

"A soda would be fine," Taylor said.

"Me, too," Petey piped in.

Matt shot a look at her and waited for her nod.

"Both of us." She gestured toward another photograph. This one was of a woman in her mid-twenties. Dressed in jeans and a chambray blouse, she stood beside a chestnut-colored horse, her face close to the animal's.

"That's my sister. Cara. She's a nut for anything Western," he said with affection.

Petey motioned toward the transformer. "Can I touch this?"

If the train had been his father's, Taylor assumed he treasured it or wouldn't have it set up. "No, don't touch, Petey."

Matt sent her a quick grin. "Sure, he can. Trains are for kids. See this." He pointed to a lever. "It switches tracks. Do it after the train goes through the tunnel."

"Okay." Petey's eyes fixed on the train running the track.

Moving closer to her, Matt realized now how long it had been since he'd invited a woman to his apartment. "Have you had lunch?" he asked but was more interested in the way the sheen of moisture had darkened her blond hair.

"Can we have pizza?" Petey yelled.

"Pizza, it is. Want to make a salad?"

Taylor realized he'd directed the question at her. "Yes—all right." *A salad.* That seemed simple enough. She followed him into the kitchen and stayed by the counter while he opened the refrigerator door and withdrew a head of lettuce from the crisper. "You said you're from Ohio?"

Matt set a tomato and the lettuce on the counter by her. "There's a cutting board here," he said, crowding her as he reached around her to open the drawer near her arm.

With an ease that amazed her, he leaned close enough not to touch her but enough to make her sway against the counter. "When did you come here?" she asked, trying to calm the nervous flutter in her midsection.

"Ten years ago." She smelled wonderful. He drew in her scent, absorbed it, whimsically wondered if it could intoxicate him.

Taylor scrambled to think about something, anything but his nearness. He'd left home. Why? He obviously cared about family. "You moved because you hated snow?" she teased.

Matt had warred with himself, wanting to kiss her. "No." He'd known another woman like her, he reminded himself. Had he learned nothing? "Loved winter," he went on, backing away. "Skiing, iceskating, playing hockey. Moving had to do with independence. I'd needed to prove myself." He set a soda on the counter near her. "My dad owned a construction business, and I'd worked for him from the time I was fourteen."

Interested, Taylor turned and lounged against the counter. She heard such affection in his voice when he'd talked about his father.

"By the time I was twenty-two, I had experience some men twice my age didn't have." He popped a beer can. "When a buddy heard about the thriving housing business going on in Phoenix, we decided to get in on it."

Matt reached for plates in a cupboard.

He recalled that time. He'd missed his family badly. He'd been so ready to meet someone, marry, start a family of his own. Unlike a lot of men in his generation, he'd always thought his life wouldn't be complete until that happened, until he had kids of his own. He'd been vulnerable, susceptible to falling in love. Now he wasn't so idealistic. Alisha had slammed reality at him. Sometimes he doubted he would ever find the right woman or have what his parents had. "Want to set the table?"

For a long moment their eyes met and held. "I thought I was doing the salad," she said.

"I'll do it." Matt handed her plates and silverware. The kitchen was too small. With any kind of movement, they were too near each other, and she was too tempting.

Not certain what was happening, Taylor wandered out of the room and sidled near Petey before setting the table. To deny she was susceptible to the man in the other room would have been a lie. She was more vulnerable with him than she'd been with any man since Justin.

"Johnny said he has a train with Big Bird on it," Petey said about a boy in his kindergarten class who he'd declared yesterday was his new friend. "But this train is better. Wait till I tell him that Matt let me do this."

"He knew you'd be careful," she said as a reminder.

"I will," he assured her.

When a knock sounded on the door, Taylor laughed in amazement. "Speedy pizza delivery," she commented and headed for the door. It opened before she reached it.

A lean, dark-haired woman breezed in, dressed in a yellow scoop-necked T-shirt and a denim jumper. She flashed a smile so like Matt's that even if Taylor hadn't seen her photograph she would have to be dimwitted not to know this was his sister. "Hi." Her smile was warm, and without words exchanged between them, Taylor felt the friendship she would offer without hesitation. "I'm Cara, Matt's sister."

Taylor returned her smile. "Taylor Elmhurst."

"You're…?"

If Taylor had blinked, she would have thought Cara's smile had been a figment of her imagination. She didn't look friendly now. Why? Nothing had happened. All she'd done was say her name.

She gave Taylor a long, steady stare. "Why are you here?"

"Why am I—"

"Cara!" Matt didn't know how much had been said, but he'd caught enough of their conversation to know Cara was about to unfairly vent anger meant for Alisha at Taylor.

Not having moved out of the doorway, he told rather than asked his sister, "Give me a hand in the kitchen, will you?" She sighed heavily, not shy about her displeasure. Matt said nothing, letting her pass him in the doorway, then followed her in and waited until they stood in the kitchen's narrow aisle.

"Okay, you're mad," she said as she swung around to face him.

"Damn straight." Inches from her, he kept his

voice low. "I love you. But who I see is my business. Don't— Don't," he said softly and slowly, "ever do that again."

Cara's back straightened. He read anger in her eyes. "Just don't get hurt again," she said in a voice as soft as his, but full of passion.

Wondering about the quietness in the other room, Taylor looked up from setting the silverware on the table to see Matt's sister at the door.

She shot a look filled with hurt at Taylor. "Sorry," she murmured in a tight tone, then opened the door to leave.

The touch of Petey's small hand brushing hers grabbed Taylor's attention. He looked as confused as she felt. "She doesn't like us."

Me, not you, Taylor mused. "Of course she does," she said, not wanting anything to spoil the day for him.

Matt strolled back in the room. What could he say to her? he wondered. His whole family had been touched by what had happened when Alisha had been in his life. He understood his sister wanting to protect him. If the roles had been reversed, he'd have felt the same way, and knowing her, she'd have resisted any interference just as he had. "Sorry about that," he said, hoping he didn't have to offer her more than the simple apology.

Head bent, Taylor fiddled with one of the forks, making much about laying it straight on a napkin. "Did I do something wrong?"

Matt could have told her, *My sister's afraid. She's*

afraid her brother will act like a dope again. "It was nothing. She thought you were someone else."

Taylor wasn't sure she understood. As he retraced his steps to the kitchen, she followed. She doubted he meant that she resembled someone. "She didn't like the woman?"

Matt gathered the salt and pepper shakers. "I was with her that night five years ago at the Crystal Hotel." Facing her, he saw questions in her eyes. He assumed she was wondering how he'd afforded dinner tickets that cost a grand each. "I was living a different life then. I met this fellow. He'd been in the construction business a long time, knew people." Matt had gotten a loan from his parents, which he'd paid back within the year. He'd been so full of big dreams back then. "I went into business with him." Harry Kerchel. Foolishly Matt had trusted the man with his life. To be fair, Harry hadn't intentionally betrayed him. "We were successful. Duran-Kerchel was rapidly becoming *the* construction company in Arizona's flourishing housing industry."

Taylor gave him a long, searching look. How could he have had so much then and nothing now?

"Then word came that my dad was gravely ill. Family always came first," Matt said with no hesitation. He took out two bottles of salad dressing and set them on the table. "I left for Ohio to be with my family. There was no reason for me to be concerned about the business. It was in Harry's capable hands." Looking back, he knew he'd been naive. He'd been raised with good values, plenty of scruples. Treat people right, his dad had always said.

Taylor discerned that he'd been hurt by someone he'd trusted.

"Phone calls to Harry, my partner, gave no clues anything was wrong." Matt took a long swallow of the beer he'd opened earlier. "Not until I returned to Arizona months later did I learn he'd financially ruined us. He hadn't been paying attention to the business," he explained. "He was enjoying the parties, the success, too much. He wasn't meeting completion dates or keeping a watchful eye on costs and construction crews."

"What happened then?"

He set down the beer can. "With the business practically wiped out, I returned to what I knew, carpentry. I'm used to working with my hands. I enjoy doing it."

A man full of pride no matter what he was doing, Taylor surmised. A moment passed before she noticed he'd stepped away to answer the knock on the door.

As Matt opened the door, Petey's *whoopee* preceded the delivery boy's announcement, "Pizza delivery."

While Matt paid for the pizza, Taylor wandered toward his shop, its back entrance adjacent to the living room. He'd talked about his past, yet he'd never said more about the woman, she realized. "Could I look around?" she asked with a glance back at Matt when he came in carrying the pizza carton. She knew better than to offend him by offering to pay for lunch.

"Sure, go ahead." A few years before, he'd begun refinishing furniture when his construction business had been slow. "Petey and I will get lunch ready," he said, aware the boy stood near in the doorway.

"Yeah, we'll get lunch ready," he echoed.

She had to smile. He seemed so content in Matt's company. Ambling into the huge room, she realized instantly that neatness didn't count. She saw a chair with a split spindle, and a fine old dresser missing an edge. A large table saw and stacks of wood cluttered one side of the room. In a far corner were intricately carved oak mantels, and on a rolltop desk was what appeared to be the claw leg for a secretary.

"It's a replacement piece," Matt said, from the doorway behind her.

"And the mantels?"

"I do restoration work at some of the old Victorians in Jerome."

And he did much more, she realized as she stepped around a partition. At the front of the store where customers would browse he'd displayed wood carvings. In fascination, she stared at one that was a foot high of a horse and its rider roping a steer. Matt Duran was a wood carver, an artist. "These are beautiful. Have you sold many?" she asked, aware he'd followed her.

"A few." There had been a man from New York who'd wanted to take as much of the West back home with him and bought enough to make life easier for him for several months and to pay off some bills.

Taylor wandered around the room. Clearly he had a love affair with wood. He built with it, refinished it, carved it. Impressed, she touched an equestrian statue. A keen artist's eye had allowed him to record vivid detail in the wood carvings.

"We're ready to eat." He tried to sound casual, but he liked seeing her here. And as her fingers stroked the statue of a galloping horse and its rider, he couldn't ignore how carefully she was touching it—as if it were precious.

With the rain falling, darkness came early. By the time Matt was driving them home, streetlights were on and rain flooded the streets. Though he braked the truck as close to the front door as possible, a dash to it left them all soaked.

His hair plastered to his head, Petey shook like a wet puppy. "I had fun today."

Drenched, Taylor raised a hand to brush away wet strands of hair from her face. She touched Petey's shoulder to gain his attention. "Why don't you go in and change your clothes."

"Okay." He tugged at Matt's hand. "Thanks for the baseball card, Matt."

Taylor watched him take off at a run into the hallway with its marble floor, doing a skid at the far end. She laughed. "He really did have a wonderful time today." She remembered after eating the pizza that Petey had dropped to his belly on the carpet to watch one of his favorite programs on Matt's television. His elbows bent, his chin propped on his palms, he'd looked the same way one time when Taylor had been visiting Jared, Elizabeth and him at their home.

Stalling, Matt ran a hand over his wet face. *What about you?* he wanted to ask. "I like him." He'd had to concentrate to answer. Unknowingly she was stirring up his juices. With the slightest movement, the snug, wet T-shirt strained against her breasts, offering a faint outline of her nipples.

"Thank you for inviting him today."

"I can't take credit." Matt thought she should know. "He called me first."

"He called?" Her laugh carried an edge of embarrassment. "I thought…" Her words trailed off as excitement she hadn't expected stormed through her. Her imagination wasn't playing tricks. At some moment, he'd inched closer.

Her heart quickening, she watched his eyes fall upon her lips. Then his hand suddenly glided down her arm. A shock wave skimmed her flesh. Taylor didn't pull back, couldn't. For hours she'd been thinking about a moment like this.

Lowering his head, Matt waited, giving her a chance to stop him, push him away. When she didn't, he slipped a hand to the back of her neck. He smelled the rain on her, tasted it as he closed his mouth over hers.

Emotions too strong to comprehend swarmed in her. Taylor melted against him, already lost in the power of his kiss. It persuaded. Seduced. She moaned, softening against him, and felt his strength, the hardness of his body, the warmth of him. Her blood pounding, she drank in the taste of him until her legs felt weak.

What she hadn't known, hadn't expected was how much she would ache for this moment or how much he would make her crave for more than his taste.

Breathless, she pulled back before she lost all will to stop him.

Matt lifted his head, wanting her, wanting to run his hands over her until they were both throbbing. Instead, he lightly traced a fingertip across her swollen mouth. But before he changed his mind and brought her against him again, he stepped back.

Taylor didn't move. The heat of his mouth lingering on hers, she watched him sprint through the rain to his truck. So what if he'd sparked desire when he kissed her. She needed to back away now before he disrupted her life.

Her heart hammering, she seized a quick breath. Sparks. How bland that description seemed. What he'd done was much more earth-shattering. He'd detonated an explosion.

Chapter Five

Matt figured this was a make-it-or-break-it kind of day. He didn't regret the kiss. Two days of reliving every second of it made him ache for more, but he concluded that today all the fantasizing he'd done since that kiss would finally be laid to rest. *Full of neat little clichés, aren't you?* he mused self-deprecatingly while unplugging his circular saw.

At daybreak, he'd driven through the security gates of her estate, hoping to squeeze a full day's work into a few hours before they left for the ball game. Now, with afternoon sunshine glaring in his eyes, he began to pack up his tools for the day.

He knew damn well that he didn't belong with her. She was champagne; he was beer. She was glitz, moneyed; he was earthy, a working stiff. She liked ballet and opera, and though he could deal with the opera, he was a country music fan. She was used to watercress sandwiches. He'd take a salami sub sandwich anyday. They were too different. But it didn't seem to matter what he knew, what made sense. He wasn't staying away from her.

From inside his truck, he pulled a clean shirt off the seat and looked across the lawn to the pool. Sunlight glimmered on the water and on her. Wearing a two-piece number in sky-blue that showed more flesh than he needed to see, she sat on the pool deck, her feet dangling in the water. And he thought again about that kiss.

He was watching her, Taylor knew. That was fair to her, since she'd been watching him, as well. While he'd worked, morning sunlight had highlighted the tinge of red in his dark hair. Shirtless, he'd glistened with perspiration, and she'd visualized a stream of moisture running down that line of dark hair just above the waistband of his jeans. Earlier, while reaching for a board, he'd turned his back to her, revealing rippling muscles.

She believed the kiss was causing all the trouble. Because of it she'd avoided him for the past few days. She'd thought if she didn't talk to him, she'd stop thinking about him. She'd been wrong. Often the sound of Petey's laughter had drawn her to the window. She'd seen Matt teaching him simple carpentry or playing catch with him.

Yesterday they'd ridden bikes down one of the desert hills. She'd heard Petey's yells of excitement whenever he'd descended the shallow incline. She would never have thought of doing that with him. Again, Matt had given him moments of fun.

On a sigh she lifted herself from the pool. Still annoyed with herself, she grabbed a towel from the chaise lounge and moseyed into the house to dress before Petey arrived home. She knew what was bothering her. She liked Matt, liked talking to him, being with him.

Standing in the bathroom, she peeled off the wet suit, then stepped into the shower to rinse off any chlorine. It had been so long since she'd felt that way about a man. But she'd learned early in life that love didn't come easily to people in her family. She knew what her parents hadn't. The one thing that money couldn't buy, that had always been out of reach was love. Since Justin, she'd begun to accept that love for her might be like an elusive brass ring, always out of reach.

Stepping out of the bathroom, she was completely dressed before she noticed the blinking light on the answering machine. Leeland usually answered the telephone, but since she wouldn't be home, she'd given him the day off. Passing by on her way to her dresser, she jabbed at the button for the message.

"Taylor, it's Ian. Where are you?" His voice held a hint of irritation. "You're never home."

Taylor U-turned to call him back.

"There's no need to call me," he went on as she reached for the receiver.

She laughed, feeling as if he was watching her.

"I'll come by later today."

At that she frowned. Quickly she punched his

phone number. On the second ring, his answering machine kicked in. Apparently he'd called from somewhere other than his penthouse apartment. With no other choice, she left a message. "Ian, I won't be home, so don't drop by. I'll call you tomorrow." They needed to have a serious talk about what wasn't going to happen.

"Matt's here," Petey yelled as he barreled in.

At the sight of his smile, she sighed with relief. Earlier he'd been annoyed with her. Andy, a playmate who used to live next door to Petey, had invited him to spend the night. Though she'd had a legitimate excuse for refusing, reminding him of the baseball game they were going to with Matt today, she hadn't wanted to let him spend the night away.

Slipping her hand around his, she knew the situation would occur again, knew she should let him go to his friend's; Jared had. But she wasn't ready for the overnight separation yet.

Smiling, with their hands linked, they approached Matt. In that instant, he accepted that he'd been waiting all morning for this moment. "Want to take the truck or your car?" he asked, when Petey broke loose to reach him.

Her head bowed, Taylor slid on her sunglasses. She'd been aware of him standing by the truck, watching her. Cowardly or not, she hid from those gray eyes, which seemed to delve too deeply. "Whatever you want."

I want to know why I can't get you out of my head.

Petey offered his opinion. "Your truck."

Taylor smiled and shrugged a shoulder. "That's okay with me."

Beside her, Petey tapped the top of his head as if searching for something. "I gotta go back. I forgot my cap, Aunt Taylor."

Watching him sprint back to the house, she wished she'd had time to stop him. She was nervous about being with Matt, especially alone with Matt. "I noticed you went bike riding with Petey. I wish I'd thought of that," she said, searching for conversation to avoid a silence. Silences with him unsettled her. Silences with him made her remember his kiss and the sensation he aroused.

"You may not thank me in a few years," Matt said lightly. "He has his eye on that hill behind the house." He rolled the sleeve of his chambray shirt to his forearm. "I told him that I'd take him down it one day."

Taylor visualized the mound dotted with straggly brush and cacti and the steep incline beyond it. "Oh, my God. That's so dangerous."

As a kid, he'd have chosen the same hill as a challenge, Matt knew. "Not when he's older."

"And after that I'll have to deal with the car issue and dating."

"Makes the hill look like a small problem, doesn't it?"

She smiled because he did, not a stingy half smile, but a full one that reached his eyes.

As the wind blew her hair across her cheek, Matt was tempted, too tempted once again to touch the silky strands. "Do you even own a bike?"

"I think you're insulting me," Taylor said good-naturedly. If she kept the mood light, kept tension between them at bay, the kiss would become a distant memory.

"No, I'm not," he said on a laugh. "But bike riding is like bowling. You don't bowl, do you?"

Taylor shook her head, growing alert to where he was going with the conversation.

"Bet you ski." With what appeared to be reluctance, she nodded her head. "I don't," Matt went on. "What else do you do?"

"Hang glide."

A smile of admiration spread across his face. "Do you really?"

She matched his smile because he looked so astonished. "Yes."

"I always wanted to do that."

"Why can't you?"

Matt shrugged. It wasn't an inexpensive sport. When he'd had the money, he hadn't had the time. "Anyway, see my point. Bike riding is ordinary." He was having a hard time not touching her again. At some moment, since that kiss, he'd begun craving for more time with her. "And the last thing you are…is ordinary." In a low, almost whispery voice, he said what he'd felt for days. "The last time you stood this close, you took my breath away."

A fluttery sensation coursed through Taylor. Was she breathing? she wondered. With his mouth hovering near, she could almost imagine his taste. When his eyes flicked to her lips, she started to look away, then he crowded her. Her heart pounding, she placed a hand to his chest. "What are you doing?"

Peripherally Matt caught movement and knew Petey was getting closer. "Nothing. At least—not now," he said close to her mouth. Lazily he dragged his gaze away from her to look down at the boy. "Guess we should go."

Petey bobbed his head. "Uh-huh. Come on, Aunt Taylor."

It took a moment to snap herself back. She stretched for a deep breath, not liking the way he tied her up in knots, not liking it one bit. Saying nothing, she turned away and crossed to the truck. Why had he said all that? It made no sense. First he'd emphasized how different they were, then he'd told her he'd been moved by the kiss. Now she was more confused than ever. If they were really smart, they would simply stay clear of each other.

Matt shouldered the way through the mob jamming the entry gates at the baseball stadium.

Nervous about the crowd, Taylor placed a hand on Petey's slim shoulder to keep him close. As someone jostled her and stepped between her and Petey, a second of panic skittered through her. "Petey." She snagged his hand to draw him near again.

Matt, too, moved closer. Aware of what had just happened, he opened his arms to Petey. "Come on. I'll give you a ride on my shoulders. Okay?"

Eagerly Petey went to him. "Wow!" Glowing with excitement, he beamed from his perch on Matt's shoulders and surveyed the crowd. Wide-eyed, he divided his interest between the souvenir booth and the snack area. "I can see lots more."

"Come this way." A hand at her elbow, Matt guided her toward the area beneath the seats. In the clearing, he lowered Petey to the ground.

"Can I have a hot dog?" Petey asked with a tug on Taylor's hand.

Since he'd moved in with her, Taylor had learned he would exist on pizza, jelly beans and hot dogs if she let him.

"I like the works," Matt said to him. "What about you?"

"Me, too."

Matt doubted that. "Onions?"

Petey made a face.

"Mustard?"

Petey shook his head.

"Relish, ketchup?"

Another shake of his head.

Matt chuckled. "Okay. One with everything and one naked. What about you?"

His face was close to hers suddenly, so was his mouth. "The works," she answered with as much steadiness as she could muster.

Feeling the heat of her breath, he nearly closed the space to her. There was going to be another kiss. And more, Matt sensed in that moment. The buzz of people, the bump of someone against his back made him give up his fascination with her mouth. "Why don't you and Petey go in," he suggested. "I'll get the food, then I'll join you."

Taylor agreed eagerly. She needed some breathing

space, a little time to stop making so much about everything that was happening between them.

Before buying the hot dogs and drinks, Matt made one stop. He'd noticed Petey had been looking longingly at the souvenirs. He might have trouble understanding his relationship with Taylor, but the boy was simple to read.

As Matt hoped, Petey was thrilled when he handed him one of the pennants. "Matt, wow! I really wanted one of those flags."

"Pennants," Taylor told him and took first the tray of drinks and then the hot dogs from Matt.

As the players were announced and came on the field, Petey hung over the railing and waved the pennant. "He winked at me," he said excitedly over his shoulder about one of the players.

Running by Petey and seeing the pennant, another player gave him a thumbs-up gesture. "Did you see that? Aunt Taylor, did you see that?"

Taylor bit back a laugh. "Yes, I saw."

He barely heard. As the game started, he never took his eyes off the field.

Time passed with relative ease. A warm breeze drifting across her face, Taylor got caught up in the game. She didn't understand all of what happened on the field, but she knew enough. "This batter is a definite out," she commented nonchalantly between bites of her hot dog.

Matt looked over Petey's head at her. "What did you say?"

"He's a sucker for the curve ball." She'd gotten that tidbit of information from an acquaintance, a sports writer at the newspaper she'd taken to lunch and pumped for information about the local team. Leaning forward, she rested her forearms on the railing as the pitcher wound up, then took a long stride forward to release the ball. The batter swung at air as the ball curved, then it whammed into the catcher's mitt. A roar of glee rose when, after two of the same kind of pitches, the batter struck out. Taylor shot a smug look at Matt. "Told you so."

Matt stared thoughtfully at her. "Know about baseball?"

"A little." She decided he didn't need to know that she'd been cramming for the past week, reading every book she could find about baseball. She wanted to believe she'd gone to all the trouble to impress Petey. But what five-year-old cared about statistics?

Matt only half believed her expertise about baseball. But what came through clearly was that she wasn't having a rotten time and didn't feel out of place. And with her scent luring him, he didn't give a damn anymore about what made sense. She'd awakened emotions in him that he'd thought he'd buried forever after Alisha.

"I had a wonderful time," Taylor confirmed when they were strolling to the truck later that afternoon. "And I ate too much." She couldn't believe she'd eaten so much junk. "And you ate more than me," she said lightly to Petey who'd consumed peanuts and ice cream and cotton candy.

He giggled before climbing into the truck. "I had fun. Can we go again?"

"You're going to be really busy with Little League starting soon," Taylor reminded him.

Matt was grateful that she'd saved him from answering. He hadn't wanted to make empty promises.

"Yeah!" Petey's eyes rounded with anticipation. "We're all going, aren't we?" He looked from her to Matt.

Matt was on the hot seat again. "When are the games?"

"We don't know yet. We have to go to sign-ups. But you can go with us and find out, too. So do you want to go with us?"

Taylor leaned forward to see around him.

Matt made the turn on to her private drive, then sent her a what-now look.

"Want to go?" she asked him.

"Want me, too?"

Something was happening here, she knew. "If you want."

As Matt cracked a smile, Petey smiled up at Taylor. "That means yes."

Amusement swept through her. "It does?"

"Uh-huh."

Matt gently elbowed him. "How do you know?"

"Because you smile when you want to say yes, but you don't say anything."

Matt chuckled. "What are you feeding him? Smart pills?"

She released a short laugh. Thinking how often Petey had maneuvered them together, she wondered if it was deliberate.

"Echo's outside again," Petey said when they

pulled up to the house. As soon as Matt braked, he unsnapped his seat belt. "Let me out, so I can get her." He was already climbing over Taylor.

She caught his arm, holding it until his sneakered feet hit the ground. His bright spirit warmed her. She hadn't seen him so happy since before he'd come to live with her. "He really loved going to the game," she said, watching him dash after the cat.

"I was surprised that you did, too. But then, you were full of surprises today."

Taylor's conscience nagged at her about misleading him earlier. "I have to be honest." She shifted on the seat to face him. "I've never been to a game before." She saw Petey playing peek-a-boo with the cat around a bush.

Matt draped an arm over the steering wheel and cast a slow, amused smile her way.

Confession was good for the soul, Taylor reminded herself. "I crammed for today, reading all kinds of books."

Humor flashed in his eyes. "I'm impressed." He was more impressed with her integrity. She didn't have to tell him. Matt thought about the ball games his father had taken his family to. Not just his brother and him. His sister, Cara, had always been included. "Didn't your father ever take you—"

Guessing what he was about to ask, Taylor shook her head, stopping him from saying more. Other fathers might do things with their children, but not her father. He'd given her and Jared everything they could want, except his company. "My father was too busy." Nothing had mattered to him but his business and making money. She stuck the sunglasses in a side pocket of her purse. "I always wondered if he was ever happy."

Silent, Matt watched a thoughtful look settle on her face. Some men lived their lives for work, excluding their family. He'd seen it before, knew marriages usually suffered then. "You weren't close to him?"

"To neither of my parents," she admitted without forethought. She frowned at the strap of her purse. How had they started talking about her family?

Curious, Matt wasn't about to let her back away from telling him more. "Why not?"

Taylor viewed the house and recalled how few times she'd laughed there before Petey had come into her life. "My mother was always busy, too. She led her own life. She wanted exactly what my father offered her. It was the reason she married him," she said bluntly. "After my father's death, she admitted she married him because he could give her what she wanted."

Matt didn't need psychic powers to guess she'd endured a lot of sadness during her childhood.

"There had never been any real love between them."

He thought about his own parents, about how often he'd seen his father's hand touching his mother's waist, or he'd noticed her smile at him because he'd done something. They'd seemed to have their own language. Silent, it spoke volumes with a look, a touch, a smile. "When did you realize this about your parents?" Matt asked, watching Petey rush toward the cat as it scooted into another bush.

"I guess I knew it when I was still young. I wasn't even home that much. I spent most of the year at boarding school. But when I was home, there was no warmth, no love. They never acted as if they loved each other. Then she simply told me."

Matt wasn't following her. "Told you what?"

"That she married him for the money. She admitted that. She also admitted that she had been miserable most of her married life."

What kind of woman shared that with her child? Matt wondered. Learning that, had she wondered if her mother cared about her? When she faced him, he stared hard at her, trying to see what wasn't visible, decipher a child's pain in the woman's eyes. He'd prodded, out of curiosity at first, then because she seemed to need someone to tell. "She could have left him if she'd wanted to," Matt reminded her, hoping to make her realize she might have misinterpreted everything.

"She couldn't divorce him."

Matt concentrated harder on her. "Why couldn't she? She'd have gotten alimony."

"She told me that wouldn't have been enough. She was unwilling to let go of all she had become accustomed to as J. Harrington Elmhurst's wife."

She'd misinterpreted nothing, Matt knew now. As she frowned again, he wanted to lean forward and touch the line marring her brow. The orange glow of sunset bathed her face.

"Money never made her happy." Taylor switched her attention to Petey, who was trying to entice the cat out of a shrub. On the fingers of one hand she could count the people in her life whose interest in her hadn't been because of the money—her aunt, two loyal and caring servants, Sarah and Petey. Ian? She wasn't sure.

Opening the truck door first, she climbed down. What about Matt? As he fell in step beside her, she knew she had to be sure she wasn't about to make the same mistake she'd made ten years ago with another man. She wouldn't be used again, wouldn't be the means to money for someone. "Why are you so willing to spend time with Petey?"

While listening to her, Matt had grown troubled with what hadn't been said. This woman had had everything money could buy, but he'd had something she'd never known. He'd had parents who'd made him feel loved. He sensed too many people in her life had cared more about money than anything else.

"I like him," Matt answered simply. He didn't think he could explain. Until the boy had come into his life, he hadn't realized something was missing. Matt hadn't expected the reaction to him, but Petey was five years old, and five years had passed since Alisha and dreams of a family had slipped from his grasp.

Taylor wanted to ask more but didn't.

"It's that man again," Petey said, suddenly beside them as a BMW drove up the circular driveway.

"A friend of yours?" Matt asked curiously because he'd heard Petey's displeasure.

Taylor wasn't sure how to categorize Ian St. John. "An old acquaintance." Among his faults was an inability to listen. She was sure he'd received the message not to come that she'd left on his answering machine and had chosen to ignore it.

"He's real bossy," Petey said with definite disgust.

Matt sent him a sidelong glance.

"And he's always putting an arm around Aunt Taylor."

"Petey—" The reprimand on the tip of her tongue remained there as Ian strode toward them. Surely it was her imagination that he'd puffed his chest. Tall, fair and immaculately groomed in his designer polo shirt and khakis, he looked as if he'd stepped off the cover of a men's fashion magazine. When he stopped a foot from them, Taylor chose to ignore his irked expression and made an introduction.

The handshake spoke volumes to Matt. He'd experienced a similar one during his adolescence, when Rod Cultin had challenged him to arm wrestle because of a cute little redhead with a saucy walk named Lauralee Jenson. Matt had won the contest and the girl. But that was almost two decades ago. He was past the age for this kind of adolescent antic. Amused, he ended the shake, then transferred the pennant and autographed baseball to Petey. "Here." As if unable to resist, he ruffled Petey's fair hair.

It occurred to Taylor how often she'd seen her brother do that, too. "We had a good time," she said. "Thank you, Matt."

All smiles, his voice smooth with interest, Ian slipped a proprietorial arm at her waist and demanded their attention with his question. "Where did you go?" He frowned at the objects in Petey's hand. "A baseball game?"

"Yes," Taylor answered distractedly. Matt had squatted before Petey to return his hug. She'd hoped for them to make some connection, for Matt to give Petey the male companionship he'd been missing since his daddy had died. She'd never imagined they would bond this much so quickly.

Matt had barely turned to leave when Ian began his interrogation. "Who is he?"

"Matt's a carpenter," Petey said too helpfully.

Ian swung a look of disbelief at her. "He's joking, of course."

"No, that's the truth." She whirled around to lead the way into the house. "Ian, why did you come over?"

"I certainly know now why you didn't want me to," he said in a peevish tone, his fingers tighter, more possessive on her arm. "Taylor, if your father hadn't died, we'd already have been married."

Annoyed with his grip, she slipped free of it. But she knew he was right. He was the man her father had chosen for her, the one he'd wanted her to marry. "Ian, you deserve someone who wants what you want. I'm not that person."

"If you'd say yes, you'd see in time that I'm right."

"Aunt Taylor?" Petey sidled close and tugged on her hand. "Can I have some cookies?"

He'd had more than his share of junk food today, but after all he'd eaten at the ballpark, she doubted he'd want dinner. Since he'd been patiently silent nearby, petting Echo again while she'd been talking to Ian, she nodded an okay.

Ian waited only until Petey had disappeared into the other room. "He's unsettled, Taylor."

He was touching her soft spot and knew it.

"He needs a family life."

Yes, he did.

"We could give that to him."

That would be sensible, what was expected of her. Everyone thought Ian was right for her. But she didn't want to marry someone just because he would give her the right life. That's what her mother had done, and she hadn't been happy. *What about love?* she wanted to ask. Why couldn't she have love?

Chapter Six

"Are you sleeping?"

Hovering at the edge of wakefulness, Taylor kept her eyes shut and her face buried in the pillow. She felt movement on the mattress as Petey settled on it beside her. "What time is it?"

"It's late," he said close to her ear. "Real late."

She moaned, yearning for a few more minutes. She'd had a difficult time getting to sleep, restless with too many thoughts of Matt, with what Ian had said. Even before he'd unwillingly left, when she'd begged off from a night out because of a headache, she'd known he was right. He could give Petey what he needed most.

Again Petey's voice sang in her ear. "Aunt Taylor."

Rolling over, she forced open one eye and squinted at him. "Is it still dark?"

Kneeling on her bed, he sat back on his heels. "No, the sun's out." Bright-eyed, he looked full of energy. "Sort of."

She remembered when she used to rise at a more civilized hour, closer to noon, and have a leisurely breakfast on the terrace. She also remembered there had been fewer smiles and laughter in her life. If given a choice, she wouldn't trade one abrupt, noisy morning with him for what she used to have.

"You gonna get up, Aunt Taylor?"

She doubted he would let her go back to sleep. She looked out the window. Drifting clouds shadowed the morning sunlight.

"We gotta go to the baseball field for sign-ups. Matt said he'd take me if you don't want to get up. Don't you want to?"

Not for a moment would she let someone else do what she considered her responsibility. But more than that, she wanted to be with him, be a part of the excitement he was feeling. "I'll be up in a few moments." With his face only inches away from her, she smelled licorice and wondered where he'd stashed the candy. "Have you eaten yet?"

"I had—" She watched his face, could almost hear the wheels spinning as he tried to answer without fibbing and not tell her about the candy.

Taylor let him off the hook. "If you haven't had breakfast yet, we can have something together."

His face brightened. "I haven't had any breakfast."

Forcing her eyes wide, she stared at the ceiling. "You go, and I'll be there in a few minutes."

He glowed with his excitement. "We gotta go soon."

"I know we do, Petey." She waited only a moment, then pushed herself to a sitting position and raked fingers through twisted strands of hair. "But we have time enough to eat."

He bounced off the mattress to stand beside the bed. "Could we eat in the kitchen?"

She plumped the pillow behind her. "In the kitchen?" The last time she'd eaten there, she'd been six.

"Matt's there. Lottie told him to come have coffee while he's waiting for us, and she asked, 'Did you eat yet?' And he said no, so she said, 'Then I'll make you something because you shouldn't go without breakfast.' And then he said, 'Don't bother.' But she said she already had cinnamon rolls made."

Taylor struggled to be more alert. "Okay. Tell him to save me one."

"I will," he shouted, and dashed for the door, chanting the verse of a favorite song about the wheels of a truck going round and round.

Joy washed over her. Do you hear the sound of a child in the house, Mother? *Yelling is unladylike,* she'd said more than once. *Walk, don't run. Play quietly in your room and close the door.*

Without Jared she would have been so lonely.

Taylor closed her eyes for a moment. For a long time, without Jared, she had been lonely. Now the grief no longer promised to erupt without any warning. But perhaps it was her loneliness for Jared that was making her so susceptible to Matt. Immediately she countered the thought. That made no sense. If she was that lonely, she would have welcomed Ian into her life. No, what was going on with Matt had nothing to do with anyone or anything else.

Aware of Petey's impatience, she moved quickly to her closet and wiggled into jeans. Within fifteen minutes, she was dressed and on her way to the kitchen. As she neared the door, she heard voices and slowed her steps.

From the other side of the swinging door, in an uncharacteristically loud voice, Leeland offered Petey encouragement. "Rev it up, Master Peter."

Shocked to a standstill, Taylor slapped a palm to her mouth to muffle a laugh. *Rev it up? Leeland?*

Quietly she moved closer, peeking in.

"Do it, Master Petey," Lottie yelled. Like Leeland, she was hunched over Petey.

On the kitchen floor with him, Matt closed a hand over a small red car similar to a blue one Petey had. "Hey, everyone's ganging up on me."

Petey giggled. "Are you ready?" His little hand folded over the top of the toy car.

"I'm ready," Matt returned. "Give us the call, Leeland."

"One…two…three…go!" the butler bellowed in his shaky voice.

Wheels spun beneath the pressure of their hands on their cars, then they raced across the kitchen floor. One stopped just short of the doorway. The other passed it and flipped over.

Matt played a sore loser. "The kitchen chair got in the way."

Going along with him, Leeland reprimanded him. "You shouldn't be a sore loser. Master Peter won—"

"Fair and square," Lottie piped in.

"Yes, quite," Leeland said. "Fair and square."

Through it all, Petey beamed from his win.

Taylor stepped in, now that they'd had their race. "I didn't know we had a raceway in the kitchen."

"I won. Did you see?" Petey asked, scrambling to stand.

As he came near, Taylor draped an arm over his shoulder. "I saw." She flashed a smile at Matt. How good he was for all of them, she realized at that moment.

At attention, Leeland assured her, "I'll get your coffee, miss."

"I have cinnamon rolls, Miss Taylor," Lottie said, looking sheepish.

Taylor wished they would both relax. Next time she would join in on their fun. "I'd love one of your cinnamon rolls, Lottie." Taylor took a seat at the table on a chair near the windows. "And a cup of tea."

Lottie looked so indecisive Taylor felt sorry for her. "Do you really want Leeland to serve you here, miss?"

Across the table, Petey hurriedly settled on a chair.

Taylor made eye contact with him. "Sometimes Petey and I will eat in here."

Petey sent her a pleased smile, making her even more convinced the cozy, relaxed atmosphere was what he was used to.

Who are you? Matt mused, leaning back and cradling the coffee cup in his hands. Alisha wouldn't have done this.

"How come I have to eat eggs and stuff?" Petey asked.

Matt winked at him. "Cause we need bigger muscles than she does."

Petey nodded with an easy acceptance of what he'd said and flexed an arm. "Like this?"

"Bigger." Matt gestured toward Petey's scrambled eggs. "Eat."

"Okay. Am I gonna get to bat today?" he asked in the same breath. He'd been eating and sleeping for this day and the sign-ups for T-ball.

"You're just signing up," Taylor said. "There won't be any batting."

Disappointment drew down his features.

"Today's important," Matt said. "They give out uniforms."

"Real uniforms? Like the kind real players wear?"

"Just like them," Matt assured him.

Taylor sent Matt a thank-you smile for handling the moment. Here was one reason why Ian might not be right for her, she reasoned. He had no idea what to say or what to do with Petey. Matt, on the other hand, seemed to have a knack for doing the right thing.

Through breakfast, Petey jumped from one subject to the next. Almost in the same breath, he switched from telling them about a big spider in the gardener's shed to his day yesterday at school. "My teacher told us the Gila monster is a giant lizard,'' he said when they were in the truck.

''Did she show you a picture of it?'' Matt asked.

''Uh-huh. They're really ugly,'' he said distractedly as they neared the parking lot adjacent to the school field. ''Do you think I can be a third baseman?''

''The coach decides that,'' Taylor told him, hoping he wouldn't be too disappointed if he had to play elsewhere.

''What if I don't like him?''

Matt decided the kid was a natural worrier. ''You'll like him.''

Straining against his seat belt, he tried to see more. ''We're the last ones to get here.''

Other cars circling the parking lot for a space assured Taylor they weren't late. ''No, we're not.''

Real anxiety colored his voice. ''But everyone is here already.''

''And so are you.'' Matt zipped the truck into a parking space.

While getting out of the truck, Taylor located the table where other children and their parents had formed a line. ''We have to go there for sign-up.'' Pivoting back to the truck, she was going to help Petey climb down.

Matt lengthened his stride to reach her in time and caught her hand in his to stop her. ''Leave him alone.''

''But—'' He said no more. He didn't need to. It became clear how close she'd come to doing the unforgivable, and embarrassing Petey in front of friends.

If she'd helped him, he would have said she was treating him like a baby. Over her shoulder, Taylor flashed a smile at Matt. "Thank you."

"I'll meet you on the bleachers," Matt said when Petey fell in step with her.

Matt watched them walk away. In her designer jeans and her Italian leather boots, she probably felt as comfortable here as he'd feel at a ballet, but she wore a smile and acted enthusiastic, all for the boy's sake.

Searching for a shady spot, Matt chose the bleachers closest to a few giant silver oaks. Sunlight glaring in his eyes, he raised a hand to shield them. Outside the fence around the field, Taylor was ambling toward the street and Ian St. John's BMW.

Matt watched them for only a few moments, then looked away. He had no right to interfere, but he'd spent the night wondering if the guy with the uptight look was her lover. Before falling asleep, he'd convinced himself she would never have returned his kiss in quite the same way, if some other man warmed her bed.

Now he wondered if that were true. Pulling away from his thoughts, he saw her zigzagging her way to him. What had St. John said, wanted? Was she regretting now that he wasn't the one who'd come with her? With another glance at the street, Matt saw that the BMW was gone.

"Petey's signed in," Taylor said, taking a seat beside him. "He's gone with his coach to get his hat and uniform."

"That guy's all wrong for you," Matt said, needing to say what was on his mind.

It took Taylor a moment to realize he was talking about Ian. At the moment she was definitely peeved at him. He'd come expecting her to leave Petey with Matt so she could join him and friends for tennis.

"You could waste your entire life with someone who never laughs," Matt said. "He doesn't, does he?"

Hardly ever, she mused, amazed at his accuracy. Looking down, she stuck Petey's birth certificate in her purse. "I don't plan to marry him. But my relationship with him is really none of your business."

"Probably not."

He looked too pleased with himself. As a smile lingered at the corners of his lips, Taylor knew now not to underestimate him. Unwittingly she'd told him far more than she'd planned.

Matt figured they would both have to make a decision soon enough about what they'd felt during that kiss.

"Aunt Taylor!" Petey charged toward them. "See my hat." He plopped it on his head and squeezed onto the bleacher between them. "It's green. So is my uniform. My coach's name is Mr. Bishop. He's nice, and there's a girl on the team who's in school with me."

"When's your first game?" Matt asked, readjusting the hat on Petey's head.

"Tuesday."

Not as cool and composed as she'd like to be, Taylor avoided those gray eyes she felt still on her, and skimmed the schedule. Hearing the excitement in Petey's voice, she vowed to check her work calendar, but planned to be at all the games.

One thought about the office led to another. As she glanced at her wristwatch, she grimaced, not believing how late it was. Mentally she calculated how much time she would need to get home, change and drive to the office. "Petey, we should go now. I have a meeting at the office."

His head shot up. "Huh? Do you have to go?" His smile had already faded. "Some of the kids are going to get ice cream."

Taylor hadn't counted on this. She'd thought she would be free by now, or she'd have never made the business appointment. "I'm sorry." She watched disappointment sweep over his face. "We'll have to go another time."

He said nothing. As a small frown wrinkled his brow, she'd have felt better if he'd fussed. Instead he grew quiet again, like he'd been during the first week after he'd come to live with her. Over Petey's head, she saw Matt's disapproval. He didn't understand, either, that she had to go.

"If it's all right, I'll take him," Matt suggested.

She hated this. She wanted to be with him, not at the office. But even though she had no choice, it wasn't fair to keep him from going just because she couldn't. "Is that all right with you, Petey?"

He shrugged, nothing more.

Taylor felt terrible.

Matt didn't need some degree in child psychology to know he ranked as only an okay substitute for her.

During the drive home, he forced the boy into conversation, hoping to recapture some of his earlier excitement. He was a good kid, polite and responsive, even though Matt could tell he was feeling low.

With a goodbye, Petey left Matt and plodded into the house. Matt strolled toward the garage, not ready to go home yet. He figured the boy might want someone to talk to, and he wanted to be there if he did. What a mess. The kid was miserable, and so was she. He really couldn't fault her. Only an idiot wouldn't have seen that she'd wanted to go with the boy.

"Mr. Duran. Mr. Duran." Huffing for breaths, Leeland ran toward him.

Matt responded to the distress in the man's eyes. "What's wrong?"

"Master Peter." He stopped to breathe.

Concerned for the elderly Leeland, Matt touched his shoulder. "Sit down. Are you okay?"

"I'm fine," he said, but he quivered with the release of a breath. "Master Peter took his bike. To that hill."

Before his last word was out, Matt took off. Swearing, he raced around the back, jumped over a hedge near the flower garden and sped for the hill. As he got closer, he heard Petey's cry.

Taylor wandered into the conference room with its highly polished table. She had five minutes until a meeting with the board of directors about the acquisition of an industrial complex. Though it was a hefty investment, Martin thought it sound, and more often than not, she relied on his good judgment.

"Taylor." A rarely heard anxiety roughened Martin's voice.

She looked up from the status report she'd been skimming and saw what she could only interpret as distress deepening the lines in his face.

"A call from your home just came in. Peter's been hurt. He's at the hospital."

"What?" For a second she thought her legs would buckle. "Oh, my God. What happened?"

He shook his head. "I don't know."

Nothing prepared her for the panic charging through her. "What hospital?"

"St. Joseph's." As she passed Martin in the doorway, he said, "I'll cancel the meeting."

"Yes, handle it."

It amazed her that she didn't get a speeding ticket. She whipped the car into the hospital parking lot, then ran toward the front entrance. Impatience and worry mingled during the elevator ride. When the doors swooshed open, she bolted and ran toward the nurses' station. "Peter Elmhurst," she requested.

"Taylor." Matt's voice spun her around.

She nearly fell against him. "Petey. Where is he?"

With a pale face and her eyes too big, she touched him with a hand that felt like ice. "He's in one of the emergency rooms." He drew her closer, but she didn't relax against him. "He's fine."

Her eyes darted around the room, along the nurses' station. "I want to see him."

"Listen, to me. Taylor, he's okay."

She needed to see him. Until she saw him, she couldn't believe anything anyone said.

"The doctor told me that nothing's broken. I didn't think there was, but I brought him here to be sure. We can be grateful that he listened and put the helmet on."

"The helmet?" She whipped toward him. "He was on the bike?"

Matt anticipated her reaction to his next words. "He went flying down the hill at the back of the house."

She sucked in a breath, trying not to let her imagination visualize what happened. "The one you said you'd take him down?"

He met the accusation in her eyes. "Yeah, that one."

Restless, needing to see Petey, she looked past him as a nurse approached them.

"The little boy is asking for someone named Matt. Is that you?"

Taylor swallowed against the twinge of hurt sweeping through her. Matt. Petey had asked for him, not her. She straightened her back. "I want to see my nephew," she said to the nurse. "I'm his guardian."

The woman glanced at Matt, then back at her. Peripherally Taylor knew Matt had nodded as if confirming the fact. "Oh." She pointed to a curtained area. "He's in there."

Taylor started forward, but halted. Something needed to be said. Long enough she'd let him shoulder a responsibility that belonged to her. "I'll be with him now. You can leave. You've done enough," she said in more of a curt tone than she'd intended. But she needed someone to blame at the moment, and he was handy.

"Tell him I was here," Matt said to her back.

Taylor hesitated on a step, but didn't look around. She knew she was being unreasonable, but she was angry at herself. She should have been the one Petey had asked for.

The nurse matched her stride. "Ms. Elmhurst? I wanted you to know that I'm sorry."

Though anxious to see Petey, Taylor forced herself to be polite and make eye contact with the woman.

"I didn't realize you were his aunt. Your nephew asked for his aunt first, but I didn't know you'd arrived yet. And your friend had brought him in, so when he'd insisted I let him know right away about the boy's condition, I—"

"It's all right," Taylor assured her before the woman continued apologizing. She gave her a faint smile and pushed back the curtain to see Petey. Her heart twisted. Seeing the right side of his face and his arm scraped from the fall, she rushed to the bed then bent over to stroke his forehead. "Petey." As he opened his eyes, somehow she veiled her distress.

He sat up and fell against her. "I'm sorry," he murmured with his face buried against her shoulder.

Tears smarted her eyes when his little arms clung to her neck as if he'd never let her go.

"I shouldn't have. Matt told me not to go there. He said don't ride the bike without me. I went cause I was mad at you."

"I know." Taylor soothed him. "I'm sorry that I wasn't there." She ran a hand over his hair, then drew him close again. *You won't be alone again. I promise.* There was just the two of them now. They had to be there for each other.

Another two hours passed before Taylor had him home. Though aware he wasn't feeling bad, she ushered him into his bedroom.

"I'm not tired," he whined, even as he scrambled into the bed.

"I know you aren't. You don't have to sleep, but you need to rest," Taylor insisted. She straightened away from the bed to see Leeland standing in the doorway.

"Excuse me, miss. Your aunt is on the phone."

"Thank you, Leeland. I'll take the telephone call in the hall." She bent forward and kissed Petey's forehead. "I'll be back."

"Can I sleep in your bed?" he asked before she reached the doorway.

Taylor paused to look back at him. "Yes," she said without hesitation, needing the closeness with him, too.

"And can I have milk and cookies?"

She laughed, guessing he was taking advantage of her mood to get whatever he wanted. "Yes. Leeland, see that he gets milk and cookies," she said in passing before she grasped the telephone receiver. "Aunt Maddie."

"My dear." Concern filled her aunt's voice. "Martin told me Peter was hurt. How is he?"

"He's fine." She was relieved to be able to say that. "He wasn't injured. Mostly scrapes and bruises."

"Thank heaven. What exactly happened?"

Taylor explained about Petey's attempt to be the next Evel Knievel on his bicycle.

Her aunt clucked her tongue. "He shouldn't have that bicycle."

"All children like to ride a bike."

"Oh, I suppose. But even if he wasn't hurt, he must have been scared. Was he alone at the hospital?"

"Actually, no. Matt found him and took him to the hospital."

"Matt?" She was silent for a long moment. "Oh, yes, the carpenter."

Before her aunt offered a repeat of her previous advice, Taylor made an excuse about needing to get back to Petey.

She walked into the bedroom to the sound of Petey snoring. Reasonably she knew she couldn't always be with him, but his accident had triggered a memory for her of when she'd been alone in a hospital.

After covering him with a blanket, she said a silent prayer of thanks for his safety. On the way to the door, she flicked off the television. The chimpanzee in the movie had been falling down the hotel laundry chute. Petey had missed his favorite part of the film.

Certain he'd be asleep for a while, she dug her keys from her shoulder bag and headed for her car. Like it or not, she owed someone an apology.

Eating humble pie wasn't fun. Once she arrived at his place, she reached over into the passenger seat of

her Mercedes and picked up the gift that she'd bought
on the way there. Gathering her courage, she slid out
from behind the steering wheel.

At the steel door that led into Matt's apartment, she
knocked several times. Thoughts of leaving assailed
her. But she planted her feet and kept knocking.

Then the door opened. He looked almost comical
with surprise.

Mentally Taylor nudged herself. It was now or
never. As nerves somersaulted in her stomach, she
swung the small bouquet of spring flowers from behind her back. "These are for you."

She'd bowled him over. Had any woman ever surprised him more? "You didn't have to," he said,
stunned.

"Yes, I did," Taylor insisted.

Feeling a little silly with the flowers in his hand,
he opened the door wider to let her in.

"I need to—to apologize."

He might have enjoyed the moment more if he
hadn't been aware of how much distress she'd been
under. Her dismissal had rankled him, but he'd
watched her hurry away and had written off her manner to nerves and anxiety about Petey. Some people
revealed their worst side when they were upset. "I've
never been given flowers before."

"Men always bring them when they want to say
they're sorry."

"I know." He'd done that often enough himself.
"Let me put these in water." She could have come
empty-handed. She could have come and never said

a word, and he would still have been pleased to see her.

Taylor trailed him into the kitchen. "I blamed you unfairly." She breathed easier now. "Why didn't you tell me what happened?"

His back to her, Matt opened a cupboard and scowled. He had no vase. What the hell would he put the flowers in? "You didn't want to hear it."

"No, I didn't." She'd been too frightened to think straight then.

With few choices, he chose a yellow plastic orange juice pitcher as a substitute vase.

"You didn't deserve the way I acted." She moved to the sink while he filled the pitcher with water. "I— it wasn't about you," she admitted, feeling foolish now. "It was about me."

Matt paused with the yellow pitcher only half-full of water and set it on the counter. Nothing had been as simple as it looked.

"I knew what Petey was feeling about being in the hospital. It was so wrong for him to be there without me." She shook her head wearily. "I was eight when I was in the hospital. I had a pain in my stomach, and started throwing up. Dora, my nanny, called my aunt, but I was alone at the hospital until she came. I remember how scared I felt."

Matt's brow furrowed. "Where were your parents?"

"My father was on a business trip in Atlanta. My mother was on a cruise in the Mediterranean."

Matt waited until her eyes met his. "What was wrong with you?"

"It was an appendicitis attack. They operated almost immediately after I arrived at the hospital."

He didn't need a genius IQ to guess that she'd been scared—alone at a hospital, in pain and scared.

Taylor remembered being in recovery, clinging to her aunt's hand. "I don't know what I would have done without my aunt. She came to the hospital."

On first impressions, Matt hadn't liked the aunt. He'd walked by her one day when she'd been visiting Taylor. She'd looked coldly at him, through him. But regardless of what she'd made him feel, she'd been a part of Taylor's life when she'd needed someone.

"She took me home." Taylor wandered to a far wall and skimmed the shelves of books—mostly mysteries and thrillers. "I was supposed to be in bed, but I heard her phone call. She asked my father what she should say to me. She expected me to ask when he or my mother, one of them, was coming home."

Which one had let her down? Her mother or father? Matt wondered.

"Of course, then I never did, so she didn't have to explain to me why neither of them came home."

Under his breath, Matt muttered a soft curse. She'd told him before about a childhood with parents too busy for their children. But he hadn't understood then how much of her own memory Petey's accident had revived.

"I really am sorry about earlier. I...I felt guilty about not being with him and needed someone to be angry at."

"You didn't have any reason to feel guilty."

"I should have been with him." She never wanted

Petey to feel alone, to believe she didn't have time for him. She never wanted him to feel unloved.

"Don't beat yourself up." Matt crossed to her. "Taylor, you can't be with him every minute. There'll be times when you're not with him."

She sent him a thank-you smile, but nothing anyone said would stop her from feeling guilty. "When I went in to see Petey, he said you told him you would be there anytime he needed you. That was nice."

"That was the truth."

"Thank you, Matt."

Curling his fingers around hers, he wanted her to know that no matter what did or didn't happen between them she had a friend. "For you, too."

As she raised her head, his eyes captured hers. "Me, too, what?"

"Anytime you need someone—" he brought her fingers to his lips "—call me."

Chapter Seven

By morning she hadn't recovered from those words. Nothing he said or did could have touched her more deeply. She couldn't remember anyone ever saying that to her. Throughout her childhood, she'd learned not to expect anything from anyone. And suddenly one man was offering to be near if she needed him. He was offering that and asking for nothing in return.

Last night when she'd returned from Matt's, Petey had been awake. He'd been still going strong, coloring in his Ninja Turtle book at nine o'clock. She'd been tired, the result of emotional stress after the trip to the hospital. She figured visiting Matt hadn't helped, either.

How ridiculous that sounded, she realized. He'd been wonderful. But thinking back, she knew Matt's sensitivity when she'd gone to see him then could be her undoing now. How had he known to offer the one thing she craved for most? Old scars had healed for her, but inside she harbored that little girl, alone and scared and yearning for love, the one who'd learned not to expect too much from anyone. And he'd given her an assurance that she didn't have to be alone.

Standing in the foyer, waiting for Petey to leave for school, she checked her watch. He was running later than usual. She assumed he'd dawdled in the bathroom, practicing the newly learned art of gargling.

As he rushed toward her with a smile, she could see where the skin on his face had been scraped during his fall. She vowed he would never look back on his childhood and feel what she had. Somehow she would do whatever she had to, change her life-style, slow down at work—anything—to provide him with the love and attention his parents would have given him.

When the limo pulled away, Taylor hurried into the house to change before Sarah arrived for their tennis game. Uncharacteristically punctual, Sarah popped into her bedroom while Taylor was still digging in a dresser drawer for her shorts and a polo shirt.

"You're not dressed."

"Nice greeting," Taylor teased. It wasn't unusual for Sarah to come up to her room without being announced. They'd been friends so long that each other's house was like their own.

Her brown hair pulled back, she stood in the doorway, wearing the tennis outfit she'd bought last week. "I forgive you." She ambled toward the mirror to check her reflection and sucked in a breath while she viewed her body profile. "What in the world happened to Petey? I passed the limo at the gates and saw him."

"He played daredevil down a hill on his bike and cost me ten years."

Sarah laughed and abandoned her reflection. "I understand parenthood does that."

Taylor yanked the white shirt over her head and tried to find her way into it.

"I heard gossip."

Taylor popped her head through the neck of her shirt. She'd never been fascinated by gossip. Quickly she wiggled into her shorts. "Which you plan to share."

"I have to." Sarah perched on the stool in front of the dressing table. "It's about you. Buffy said she saw you going in to a Cave Creek diner several weeks ago."

Bent forward to retrieve a sneaker, Taylor snapped to a stand.

"It wasn't about just you."

Taylor settled on the edge of the mattress and shoved on her shoe. "Would you please tell me what you aren't saying?"

"Corey Renault—"

Taylor's interest waned. Corey was not a reliable source. She gossiped about anything and everything, often relaying more what her imagination had conjured up than fact.

"She was practically beside herself. She elbowed me and said that Buffy, too, recognized him."

Taylor finished tying her shoe. "What are you talking about?"

"Your carpenter. Matt." Sarah vacated the stool. "They both know him."

"Corey and Buffy?"

"They've met him. You aren't going to believe this." Sarah plopped on the bed beside Taylor. "Corey said that he used to be Alisha Marscroft's significant other."

Taylor stilled in tying her sneaker. She couldn't brush aside the information as something Corey had dreamed up. Matt had told her that he'd had a successful business. Was Alisha Marscroft the woman he'd been talking about?

"Can you imagine?" Sarah released a short laugh. "Alisha Marscroft and a carpenter."

"He used to own a construction company."

"So it's true?"

"I don't know," Taylor answered while she tied her shoe.

"How could he fall for her? She's such a phony," Sarah said with distaste.

But she knew how to charm, Taylor recalled. A tall, willowy brunette, she could work a room, captivating people. She was beautiful, enchanting, personable when it suited her. Though Taylor had worked only briefly with her on a committee, she'd had enough association with Alisha to know they'd never be friends. Shallow and self-centered best described her. She'd done little work on the committee but had shown no hesitation to take enormous credit when the fund-raiser proved successful. No, Taylor hadn't liked her.

"I wondered what happened."

She had no idea. Matt had left out that part of his past when he'd told her about his business.

Sarah turned a questioning look at her. "Are you dating him?"

Taylor handled the question as humorous, aware of her friend's ability to home in with startling accuracy on what was left unsaid. "Hardly."

"But you've gone places with him."

"For Petey. I told you." Again she capsulized the agreement she'd made with Matt about Petey.

"So you've gone to a baseball game."

Taylor nodded, deciding not to mention the day at his apartment.

Affectionately Sarah placed a hand on Taylor's shoulder.

"Let's approach this differently. You obviously do think he's—what he is—gorgeous, don't you?"

"Mel Gibson and him. But do you remember a previous conversation we had when you told me your mother would faint if you brought someone like Matt home?"

"That's me, not you. You don't have my mother."

Taylor smiled at the seriousness on her face.

"So the big question is are you planning to accept Ian's proposal?"

Instantly Taylor frowned. "I don't love him."

Sarah pulled a face. "I doubt if that's a necessity to him. You'd make a perfect wife to handle business dinners. That's what he's looking for."

What about me? she wanted to say. "Simply said. Usefulness is my finest asset." She'd always done what was expected of her, hadn't she? But marriage? How could she marry Ian? Why was she seesawing about this? She didn't want history to repeat itself, didn't want to be miserable like her mother had been in a loveless marriage. How could Ian be right for her? He didn't excite her. She didn't think about him when she wasn't with him. But Petey needed a father. And Ian was offering marriage, a family life, all that she needed to give Petey.

"If you feel that way, then—" With Sarah's speculative sound, Taylor focused on her. "Why can't you enjoy yourself with whomever?"

Oh, how easy she made that sound, Taylor mused. "Let's go," she insisted to avoid answering her friend. Couldn't Sarah see the problem? What if she fell in love with Matt? Already he'd touched her with his tenderness, with a kindness she'd never expected.

At the doorway Sarah hooked her arm with her own. "You're not going to answer me, are you?"

To divert her, Taylor preyed on her sweet tooth. "If you're willing to play long enough to work off calories, I'll tempt you with some of Lottie's fabulous pecan rolls."

"Not fair. You know my weaknesses, how to distract me." She preceded Taylor outside. "By the way, do you want to make it a foursome Friday night for your birthday? I thought we'd have dinner at Blair's in Scottsdale," she said about a must-be-seen-at restaurant that had recently opened.

"Fine," Taylor answered, but the big question was who would be her partner in that foursome?

Sunlight glared off the chrome fender of Matt's pickup truck. Squinting, he reached into the truck bed for a sports drink from his cooler.

Earlier while he'd been sawing a two-by-four, he'd heard female voices and laughter. From where he'd worked, he'd seen Taylor and her friend. Sarah, he remembered, was her name. Unable to resist, he'd watched Taylor respond to a volley, her legs smooth and tight below the white shorts, her face glowing with perspiration.

Now while he finished the last of a ham and cheese sandwich, he saw her with Petey. Again she showed too much leg for his peace of mind. This time a pair of worn-looking denim shorts snugly curved around her backside.

Looking deadly serious, Petey wound up and tossed a ball at her. As the ball smacked into her mitt, delight flashed across his young face. "Was that a good one?"

"It was super," Taylor called out.

She was changing. Weeks ago, she'd told him she couldn't do that, wouldn't even try. She even looked different, Matt thought. Cute. He supposed that's why he found her fascinating. Sometimes she looked like a high-society princess, and then other times, with the boy, her hair tied back in a ponytail and swinging out of the back of a denim-colored baseball cap, she looked like a teenager.

"Petey, that's wonderful," he heard her yell about Petey's last throw.

Looking pleased, Petey beamed.

Matt turned his back on them, fighting an urge to join them. Half an hour, then forty minutes passed and he was still struggling to work, constantly distracted by them. By her, he mused.

From the top of a ladder in the half-built garage, he watched her walking along the brick path as a car braked in the driveway. Some Mediterranean-looking guy, the dark, suave, sophisticated type, in a fencing outfit, emerged from the sporty coupe and flashed a mouthful of white teeth at her. An annoyance burned in the pit of his gut. Instantly he recognized what it was, and he wasn't crazy to feel it. He'd never felt jealousy before about any woman, not even Alisha.

Efforts to brush the emotion aside failed. Before he left for home later, the jealousy hit again. Matt knew he had no rights. That didn't seem to matter.

Dressed to the nines in something glimmery and slinky in black, her hair caught up off her neck by two silver combs, she left in a Saab with a guy who'd looked like a corporate lawyer.

Matt swore under his breath while he packed up his tools. He wished he'd gone home earlier. Mostly he wished he'd missed the sight of her with other guys.

Taylor assumed a thirtieth birthday was a turning point in a person's life. But Friday morning she awoke feeling no different from the day before. Showered and dressed, she entered the kitchen, guessing she would find Petey there. He seemed to prefer the homey atmosphere, the breakfast clatter.

As she laid a palm against the kitchen's swinging door, she was greeted with singing.

"Happy birthday to you, happy birthday to you."

Touched, Taylor smiled at the group of three serenading her.

"Happy birthday," Petey yelled, rushing to her. She bent over to receive his hug and kiss. At the stove, Lottie beamed, and, waiting to serve, Leeland grinned. This was her family now, she realized. People she cared about, who cared about her. Her aunt, out of town, had called at daybreak with a birthday phone call, having forgotten time differences. Taylor hadn't minded the early wake-up. There had been birthdays when her aunt had been living in Europe, when Jared had been barred from the house, when no one except Lottie and Leeland had been around to celebrate her birthday.

"I made your favorite. Blueberry pancakes," Lottie said now, snapping Taylor from thoughts she decided were meant to be forgotten.

"That's wonderful." She looked down at Petey's homemade card with its crude drawing of his favorite subject. This time he'd drawn a yellow and orange truck. It was the most beautiful picture she'd ever seen, she decided when she opened the folded paper to the words shakily printed, "I love you. Happy Birthday."

"Thank you, Sweetheart," she said and leaned down to kiss his cheek. "I love my card."

"I made this, too. It's a paperweight."

It was an irregular square of clay, painted a purplish blue and dabbed with one yellow dot of paint and one red one. "It's beautiful. I'll take it to my office."

He glowed with pleasure from her praise.

She thought this might be one of the best birthdays she'd ever had. What more could she want than three caring people with her, her favorite breakfast, the sound of clanging pots and running water, and the aroma of coffee brewing drifting on the air?

Across the table from her, Petey entertained himself by chasing doughnut-shaped cereal through the milk with his spoon. "But you gotta free the crab," he was telling Lottie about a new software game. Last night they'd watched several cartoons, then they'd played the computer game.

Lottie swiveled her head to send a look over her shoulder. "How do you do that?"

"You gotta get a key from the eel," Petey said about the neon green animated creature on the software game. "But you can't get the key from the eel until you feed it the peanut butter and jelly sandwich. You get that from the little fish's grandmother."

Taylor could imagine her mother's aghast expression if she'd witnessed this scene. "It's a sweet, well-rounded looking flounder with glasses," she told those interested in knowing, which seemed to be both of her loyal servants.

"Then you can free the crab." His eyes bright, he looked at Taylor. "We did it, didn't we, Aunt Taylor?"

"Yes, we did."

"At school one of the girls has a pet crab and a talking bird. Could we get a bird?"

Taylor looked up to see Lottie's eyes dancing with amusement. "I don't think Echo would welcome it."

He frowned at his cereal as if considering what she'd said. "What about fish?"

"Maybe when you're bigger."

"I told Matt about the bird. He said that when you have one you have to clean its cage."

"Did he have one?"

"No. He said he had a dog." He made a slurping sound as he took in the last spoonful of milk. "It was a shepherd." He grew quiet as if trying to think of something. "A-Aus—"

Taylor made a guess. "An Australian shepherd?"

His face lit with a smile. "That's it." He dabbed a napkin at his milk mustache. "Rufus."

Taylor smiled at the name of the dog.

"He used to have to feed it."

"When you have pets, you have to care for them."

"That's what Matt said. He said he didn't mind. His brother had to walk it. And his sister had to make sure it always had water."

Interested, Taylor propped an elbow on the table and rested her jaw on her knuckles. She'd had no idea he had a brother. Looking out the window, she saw Matt standing beside his truck and talking on his cell phone. What else didn't she know about him?

Matt listened to his sister's woes about her car, then agreed to take it to the mechanic. He eyed the present for Taylor that he'd placed on the passenger's seat in his truck this morning. He wouldn't have known it was her birthday if Petey hadn't let it slip during a brief conversation several weeks ago. After he'd decided on what to give her, he'd pried Lottie with questions until he'd learned Taylor had loved the color lilac since she'd been a small girl.

Matt had gone to the store and bought the biggest lilac bow he could find to match the color in the small flowers on the wrapping paper. An experienced Christmas present wrapper, he even spent time running a satiny ribbon diagonally across the present.

"Matt?"

He snapped himself back to his sister.

"Why did you miss dinner at Tom's the other night?"

He'd expected this question. The third Monday of every month, he and Cara went to their brother's house for dinner and a night of playing some board game or watching the hottest new video. "I was at a ball game." He'd left a message on his brother's answering machine, saying that he wouldn't make it. Matt knew one of them would need a more detailed reason.

"Did you go with *her?*" Cara asked.

"Yeah, with her." A woodpecker tapped away at a nearby tree. A gentle breeze rustled leaves. Sunlight glaring in his eyes, he squinted and shifted away from it. "You don't know her."

"You like her?"

Oh, hell. "Yes, I like her, Cara."

As she groaned softly, he figured he needed to set her straight about Taylor. She wasn't Alisha, she wasn't anything like her. "I'm helping her with her nephew."

"Her nephew? There's a boy involved in this?" She was silent for a moment. "The little boy who was at your place?" she asked.

"That's him." He rested his backside on the edge of the dropped tailgate again. "He needs people who care about him. If he's willing to let me be one of those people, I'm going to be there for him." Matt knew that eventually she would understand. She was a real softy. He also knew how much she wanted to protect him. She couldn't do it. That's what she didn't understand.

"It wouldn't do any good to offer advice, would it?" she asked, giving an uneasy laugh.

"You're a smart lady."

"Oh, puleeze." She moaned about his compliment, but Matt knew it pleased her. "What about the aunt?" she asked.

"I'm not going to marry her."

"But you plan to do something."

"I really love these conversations with you. Do I ask about your sex life?"

"No, but—"

"Stop worrying," he answered distractedly, visually following Taylor as she strolled along the cobblestone path in the flower garden. He stared at her slender back, at the glistening strands of her hair beneath the sunlight. One thought filled his mind. He wanted her. Not just physically. He wanted her in his life. He wasn't looking for anything permanent, but he sure wanted her. "Say goodbye," Matt urged his sister while he snatched up the birthday present from the truck seat.

With it in his hand, he ambled across the lawn to her. As she snapped off a dried-up blossom from a cluster of flowers, Matt stopped a few steps from her. "Happy birthday." She spun around, looked surprised.

Taylor blinked at the gift he'd brought around from behind his back. Astonished he'd gotten her something, she almost said something truly dumb about the present such as, "For me?" A large, square-shaped gift, it was beautifully wrapped in white paper with clusters of tiny lilac flowers and a gigantic bow. "Petey told you?"

"If you had a secret, I wouldn't share it with him."

Taylor set down the basket of flowers she'd picked and accepted the present from him. She balanced the box on the edge of the nearby fountain, and slowly undid the wrapping paper.

Had she ever just torn paper from a present? Matt wondered, amused.

Not for the first time, he'd moved her. Her heart thudding so loudly she was surprised he couldn't hear it, she peeled away the last of the wrapping paper, then lifted the lid off the box. A carving of a horse standing on its hind legs was nestled in lilac-colored tissue paper. Taylor realized then nothing had been left to chance. He'd taken time to learn her favorite color and to learn about a dear memory. "Matt. It's beautiful," she said about the statue. "It looks like—" She paused and met his eyes.

"I remembered that you said you never had a pet.

But Lottie told me you used to go riding at a nearby stable.''

"It looks like—Passel," she said about the sleek black horse that she'd loved to ride.

Matt was pleased. He'd gone to the stable, learned she rode only one horse whenever she came there. "At the stable I saw a photo."

Her heart felt as if it was in her throat. Looking down, she ran her fingertips over the smooth finish of the sculpture. The horse she'd ridden those many years ago had felt just as sleek. "I rode that horse every day through the summer for two years. I was heartbroken to leave it when my parents sent me to boarding school in Switzerland. And when I came back at Christmas break, I learned he'd been sold to some man."

Matt waited a moment until she looked at him. "So it got a home?"

"A good one." Taylor smiled now with the memory. "After I left, another girl began riding Passel. Her father bought him for her."

Had she wished she'd been that girl? Matt wondered. Had her parents even been aware of how much she'd loved that horse?

As he brushed his knuckles lightly across her cheek, pleasant tension slithered through Taylor. For her he'd gone to the stable to find out about a horse that had been part of her past when she was twelve. Again he'd touched her. Not for the first time he'd made her feel special. Pressing a hand to his chest, she leaned closer to brush her lips across his. "Thank you so much."

Matt saw the delight in her eyes. As the softness of her lips met his, he let her lead, accepted the brief, sweet kiss, but he wasn't ready to let her go. "You're driving me crazy," he murmured. He pressed his mouth to her temple. "I can't stop thinking about you."

Pleased only brushed the surface of what Taylor felt. "Is that bad?"

Placing his palms at the middle of her back, he drew her tighter against him. "That depends." Nothing between them was simple. Eventually they'd go their separate ways. So why even start something that couldn't be finished? The answer came easily. Because with each deep breath he took, her fragrance teased him. Because in the middle of a conversation with someone, he would think of her. Because it was her face, her voice, her laugh that he couldn't forget.

Slowly, so slowly that she felt caressed, his eyes raised from her lips. "On what?"

"On whether or not you can't stop thinking about me."

He'd come amazingly close to pinpointing exactly what was happening. But all the warnings Taylor might think of later failed to form as his mouth fastened on hers. She wanted to think clearly. How could she? With a kiss he was reaching a sheltered part of her heart. In seconds, he kindled warm pleasure through her. He made her blood pound, her pulse quicken, her body heat.

Matt heard her soft moan when he started to draw back. It took effort to think, to get past the taste of her. Sweet. Promising. Inviting.

With fascination he touched some strands of hair near her cheek. "I won't make you any promises, Taylor." He'd never had this kind of conversation before, but he wanted everything spelled out with her. He wanted no regrets, no pain when they ended it.

"I didn't ask for any promises," she said with a calmness her thudding heart belied. Did he think she didn't know they were wrong for each other? Of course they were. That didn't seem to matter. She stared at his mouth and wasn't able to think about anything but the pleasure she'd found in his kiss.

Matt made himself let go of her arms. "Be sure. Think about it." He sure as hell would, he knew. He accepted the desire that raced through him. What knocked him for a loop was how lousy he'd felt all morning without her, how much he'd missed her, how different he felt now because she was near.

Chapter Eight

Matt had decided to take time off from work, but he felt restless. He figured she needed to think about what he'd said. So for the past two days he'd stayed away from the house.

Slouching on the sofa in his living room, he chomped on his third doughnut. An explosion and several gunshots blared from the action-adventure movie on the television. With unseeing eyes, he stared at the screen. He'd read the newspaper, done the morning crossword puzzle, read several chapters of the latest thriller by a bestselling author, and it was only one in the afternoon.

Lacking even the ambition to move, he toed off his sneakers, then stretched out on the sofa. He was just out of sorts, tired. He'd awakened at five that morning, and even before rolling out of bed, he'd felt annoyed.

As the morning dragged on, he'd dodged an impulse to call her. He'd jogged, running himself ragged before he'd returned home and collapsed on the sofa. He'd barely moved for several hours.

He'd meant what he'd said to her, believing they needed the ground rules, needed to understand that nothing long-term would happen. But hadn't he really said the words more for himself than her? He couldn't afford to forget what wouldn't happen.

He'd told her that he wanted no promises. He believed she wouldn't want them, either. Like him, she recognized that they came from two different worlds. It made no sense to try and blend them.

But why couldn't they take some time for each other for a little while? That's what he'd been too dumb to accept with Alisha. No more. With Taylor he knew that the time with her was limited. Whatever they found together wasn't meant to last. This time he knew the score, knew what to expect and what would never happen. And this time he wouldn't play the fool.

Weary after a morning of answering phone calls regarding business, Taylor set the receiver in the cradle and resolved not to pick it up again. With her coffee cup cradled in her hands, she heard a familiar sound and stared out the opened terrace doors at the gardener riding the lawn mower. It seemed so long ago when business was all that mattered to her.

That was before Matt had swept into her life and

tempted her with something she wasn't sure she wanted. Justin had been the last man in her life. Though her father hadn't approved of him, she'd thought he was wrong. But J. Harrington Elmhurst rarely made mistakes. To prove it, her father had taped a conversation he'd had with Justin. If he made it financially worthwhile, would Justin relocate, leave Taylor alone? Her young heart had broken in seconds when she'd heard the tape. He hadn't even hesitated. Whatever her father had said, he'd agreed with.

Since then she'd been with men for companionship, like Ian and a cousin of Sarah's. Most recently she'd attended a business meeting at a board member's home the other night. The board member had completed the foursome for her birthday dinner because his fiancée, a lovely cellist whom Taylor had met and liked instantly, was out of town. But she'd honestly begun to believe she would never feel anything for any man again. She was wrong, she knew now, wandering to the window to look for Matt. A pang of disappointment coursed through her that he hadn't changed his mind about taking time off from work. Maybe it was just as well. She needed more time to think clearly.

No longer hearing the sound of the lawn mower, she roused herself from the sofa and wandered in to Petey's room to see what he'd packed for his sleepover at his friend's house. Having successfully quelled her misgivings about letting him go, she stepped in to see him sitting on the floor with his duffel bag between his spread-out legs. "Did you pack your toothbrush?"

He jammed a Godzilla comic book into the bag. "I did."

She noted he'd also packed his green plastic snake, the 3-D glasses he'd gotten from a cereal box the other day and several other comic books.

With the beep of a horn, he hustled to his feet. "Got to go." He flew at her.

As his arms coiled tightly around her neck, she laughed and squeezed him. She was grateful he still enjoyed snuggling. "I love you."

"I love you."

"I love you more," she said, leading him in to a familiar game.

"I love you more."

Taylor laughed, giving him one more quick hug. "Beat you to the door," she teased, and released him.

He was giggling when he made it there a step ahead of her.

Within a few minutes, his friend Andy and his mother and Petey drove away. Standing at the front door, Taylor waved goodbye, already missing him.

"Are you sure you don't want me to stay, miss," Lottie asked from the kitchen doorway.

Taylor walked toward her. "No." As Lottie stepped back, Taylor went in. "I can heat up dinner."

Shaking her head, Lottie clucked her tongue while she gathered her sweater and purse from a utility closet. "I don't feel right about that."

Amused, Taylor moved behind her and affection-ately touched her shoulders. "Have a good time with your sister."

Lottie muttered a goodbye, hesitated, then left. Earlier she'd talked excitedly about the play, a first for her, that she and her sister had tickets for.

Grabbing her purse, Taylor left the house, too. She planned a night of eating dinner while watching a video, and later, finishing the latest medical thriller she'd started weeks ago.

At the video store, she chose a romantic comedy featuring Meg Ryan and purchased a bag of microwave popcorn. Even a kitchen novice like her should be able to make popcorn.

Back home she changed into a knee-length nightshirt with Garfield on the front of it, then wandered in to the kitchen. Leaning against the counter, she read Lottie's directions on how long to heat the small casserole of lasagna. It seemed easy enough. All she really had to do was hit a couple of buttons on the microwave.

Though being alone had never bothered her before, tonight the silence in the house made her edgy. The reason was simple to understand. She'd become accustomed to noise, people. She was missing Petey. And Matt.

Not the most sensible thought, she knew. She thought of the complications if she got more involved with him. Whatever they started wouldn't last more than a few weeks. He'd told her, hadn't he? No, he'd warned her that there would be no ties. The problem was his kiss. When he'd kissed her, she'd forgotten everything.

At the ding of the microwave, Taylor removed the casserole. On a sigh over her own conflicting thoughts, she reached in a drawer for a spatula. Her fingers never closed over it. A sound, nothing more than a squeak, stilled her. Even as she didn't move, she shot a look around for something to defend herself with. Then she heard another squeak. Her heart pounding, she grabbed the spatula and whirled around. Matt stood in the doorway of the servant's bathroom.

"What the hell are you doing?" he asked, a towel in his hand. He couldn't help but laugh at the sight of the spatula in her hand, raised high in the air.

Taylor drew a few deep, calming breaths. "You scared me silly. I didn't know anyone was here."

"Sorry." With a thumb, he gestured behind him. "I was washing up before I left. Where is everyone else?"

"Petey's at Andy's, Leeland's visiting his brother. He's in the hospital."

"I'd heard." He smiled slowly and swept a lengthy look down her knee-length nightshirt. "He's better."

"Yes." A closeness had developed between him and everyone in the household, she realized. "And Lottie's seeing a play, *Pygmalion.* I didn't think you were coming today." She'd checked all day for him, though.

"I had a few small jobs to do." Actually he'd been going crazy at home, wanting to see her. But when he'd arrived, he'd seen some discarded wood and had cleaned up the mess first, piling the boards in the back of his truck.

He'd walked to the house to clean up, but not until stepping in the empty, quiet kitchen, had he remembered this was Lottie's night out. "What did you cook?"

"Lasagna." The ball was in her court, she knew. "Do you want to join me?"

He would eat Italian food anytime. In fact, he'd been known to heat pizza for breakfast. "It's a favorite of mine." When she turned her back to him, he stepped close behind her, crowded her.

Nerves danced with his nearness, with the touch of his fingertips on her hip points. "Is it?"

"Uh-huh." Light as a feather Matt pressed his lips to the side of her neck. He felt no resistance, knew he wouldn't leave unless she made him. "I have an aunt who dated this guy, a Pavarotti lookalike." He paused to nibble her ear. This closeness with her was what he'd been longing for. "He'd burst into song whenever there was a lull in the conversation."

Over her shoulder, she smiled, wondering if he was making up a story. "An exaggeration?"

"No, it isn't." His eyes danced with humor. "Someone would say, 'Is it going to rain?' and he'd sing back the weather report."

She laughed. "Colorful character." A little uncertain where they were going, she slipped around him. "So what does this have to do with the lasagna?"

"He was a great cook. And a lot of fun," Matt said, willing to give her space for a little while. "Whenever he invited us over for ravioli or spaghetti or whatever he'd decided to make, he would sing an aria to his captive audience."

Taylor opened the refrigerator for the wine. "What happened with the romance?"

"She met a banker and married him. I thought she made a giant mistake."

She angled a smile at him. "You have a big family, don't you?"

He would like her to meet them, he realized. "Only my parents and brother are here. And my sister."

She was envious. When he'd been telling the story, what had come through was the affection and laughter they all shared. "Do you want wine?"

He wanted her. "I'll open it."

Taylor handed him the bottle she'd retrieved from the refrigerator before she swung away to remove the casserole from the microwave. With a glance back, she scanned the cupboards. "I think wineglasses are in that one," she said, pointing.

Matt opened the cupboard she'd indicated. It held plates. "Wrong one."

"Try—" She noticed he was already opening another one.

"Found them." He'd imagined a lot of moments with her during the past weeks, but never one like this. Her life-style was similar to Alisha's, but not once had he stood in the middle of the kitchen at the Marscrofts' palatial home with Alisha.

"I—" Taylor went silent as she noted a tensing in his features. For a moment he hadn't moved. He stood so still—his eyes distant as if he were lost in his own thoughts. "Is something wrong?"

Matt shook away thoughts of Alisha. "I was thinking about someone I knew years ago."

Taylor dished lasagna onto plates. "A woman?"

In his opinion, only a jerk would admit that to another woman. "Skip it. It's not important."

She had to probe. He knew about her past, about the sadness in her youth. Fair was fair. Something had happened or he wouldn't keep cleverly avoiding any discussion about Alisha. "Someone told me you know Alisha Marscroft."

That he'd been linked to her by one of Taylor's friends seemed predictable. He'd gone to polo games, charity functions and private dinner parties with Alisha. "A woman from my past," he said with a lightness he knew instantly she wasn't buying. Her blue eyes pinned him, trapping him for more of an explanation. "I met Alisha when she came by a construction site. My crew was working on a building for her father. She and I were all wrong for each other."

Taylor heard the real meaning behind his words. *Like us.*

"But we started seeing each other. I was successful." For a while he'd believed their backgrounds didn't matter. Back then he could give her the life she was used to.

"Did you love her?"

"I guess I did," he admitted grudgingly. He'd thought she was perfect. Matt uncorked the wine. "I had to go to Ohio because of my dad's sickness. I missed her, wanted her to come meet my family. Everyone was living there back then." He poured the pale pink wine into the fluted glasses. "But she always had a reason why she couldn't come."

Matt set the wineglasses on the table. "When I returned, I learned what my partner had, or rather, what Harry hadn't done,'' he said, recalling the irate calls because deadlines weren't being met and bills weren't being paid. He'd felt as if his world had been caving in. ''It became clear my life-style was about to change, so Alisha called it quits.''

Taylor offered a slim smile as he held out her chair for her. He'd said that with such indifference. She didn't believe it for a minute. ''Why?'' she asked when he'd settled on a chair.

''You more than anyone should know what really went wrong. Would your father have approved of a carpenter calling on you?'' He released a mirthless laugh. ''Her father hadn't. He said I would never belong in her world. I wasn't good enough for Adam Marscroft's fair-haired daughter. I didn't believe she thought that. Why would I? She'd said she loved me. She acted like she did.''

Matt didn't bother to sugarcoat it to save his pride. He wanted her to understand he wouldn't make the same mistake twice. ''She'd said it had been fun, a great adventure with someone her father would never approve of.''

Taylor poked a fork in the noodles. The lasagna was creamy, spiced with oregano and basil, but she swallowed the food in her mouth with difficulty. Was she understanding him correctly? Alisha Marscroft had admitted that she'd been with him for kicks? She'd taken his heart and had pierced his pride just to defy her father? ''You think I'm like her?'' He gave her a long, searching look, but was silent. His quietness hurt her more than a dozen words could have. Taylor stood, needing a few seconds away from his gaze. Then she could meet his stare and he wouldn't see just how much he'd hurt her. ''I'm not her.''

Before she'd taken two steps from the table, Matt blocked her path. ''I know you're not.'' He caught her chin to hold her face still. His gut was tight, a yearning to pull her against him so obvious that she would have to be stupid not to feel it. To be with this woman, he needed to bury memories of Alisha.

Taylor knew the doubts, the conflict within herself and him. But as he pulled her closer, she swayed against him, her mouth meeting his. With the world outside the room not a part of the moment, she didn't want to think about consequences. Feelings washed over her of how this moment was meant to be. Placing a hand against his chest, she felt his heart thudding in the same quickened beat as her own. ''Do you want to make love with me?'' she whispered against his lips.

That was the one question Matt knew he couldn't say no to. ''Want?'' He whispered words to her. ''I'm aching to make love with you.''

They never made it past the living room. With her arms curled around his neck and her lips fastened on his, desire he'd only fantasized about became reality. He twisted his mouth across hers and curved her softness into him. He wanted to tell her that she was opening his heart again, but he couldn't say the words aloud.

She was greedy for him, Taylor realized, her heart pounding as if she'd been running for her life. The lips playing over hers left her breathless. She heard his moan and her own. She knew no logic in what was happening between them. She only existed for her feelings. She tasted passion, seduction, a thoroughness in his kiss that was meant to snatch away her breath.

He was succeeding. She trembled beneath the caress of his fingers near the rounded edge of her breast. She tingled. She burned. Whatever he wanted, she would give. Nothing mattered except the taste of his mouth.

Needs building, she tugged his shirt from his jeans. ''Matt.'' His name came out on a whisper as he drew her nightshirt off first one shoulder and then the other. Material shimmied down to her waist. Impatience nudging her, she popped the snap of his jeans, and with the heel of her hand, she shoved the denim away from his waist. On a groan, he pulled her to the floor with him.

Lost in longing, she pushed at his shirt, urging him to pull it off. A moment, no more than two, passed before his bare flesh brushed against hers. The chill of night danced across her skin, yet only the heat within her body mattered. She grew wild beneath his touch when, with persisting slowness, as if memorizing every inch of her, his lips glided over her body, his tongue moistening and stroking it until she was nearly mad with feelings.

All Matt had imagined paled in comparison. With his mouth, he explored the smoothness of her belly, the leanness of her rib cage, the soft curve of her breast. He heard her sigh as his mouth moved downward, as he found soft, hot inner flesh.

He maintained command only until she touched him. She taunted his control with gentle soft caresses, with the slow rubbing movement of her body. She tore his breath from him, her hands eager and greedy roaming over him, stroking him until he was throbbing.

On a gasp he turned away, sought the foil packet in his wallet. With his hands not quite steady, he succeeded in opening it. Protection in place, he leaned over her again.

As her mouth searched his, his met it. His heart pounding, he pulled her arching hips closer. He was beyond anything he'd ever experienced before. He stared into eyes clouded with pleasure, watched them close. As if inviting, her legs curled to hug his hips. Slowly Matt slipped into her.

A rhythm began, steady and even, then more frantic. Flesh melded. Heat flowed. He rode sensation, drowned in it, until it was all he was, until sanity slipped from his reach, until the world as he knew it was her, only her.

Time stopped. For a long moment Matt was still struggling to breathe. He listened to the rain pelting the window while he waited for his heart to slow to a normal beat. Despite the mantle of darkness, he could see her face, soft and smiling. Satisfaction he hadn't believed possible filled him. Dazed, he wondered how such closeness had come so quickly. "Taylor—"

Her fingertip touched his lips, silenced him.

"Stay," she murmured against his shoulder. She didn't need words. She wanted him.

Matt tightened his hold, then rolled to his back, keeping her with him. He didn't want to think too much. With her length stretched against him, he fingered strands of her hair. He saw passion in the blue eyes, darker than usual. Then she moved over him, bracing herself above him. Blood pounded in his head when she scooted down, when her mouth covered him. "You make me breathless," he murmured. An ache surged through him, consuming him. He closed his eyes, concentrated on the sound of the raindrops and knew he would never experience another rainy night and not remember the thrill, the excitement, the contentment he felt during this one.

It wasn't the warmth of morning sunshine that made Taylor open her eyes, but the emptiness beside her. She didn't need to look, to reach out to the mattress to know he was gone. With unbelievable swiftness, disappointment spiraled within her.

Had she been fooling herself, believing his feelings for her went beyond sex? It wasn't that he hadn't been fair. If she was hurting, that was her own fault, wasn't it? She shouldn't have expected more than a night. But she'd wanted more. Much more.

Her spirits down, her eyes closed again, she gave thought to staying in bed all day with her head buried under the pillow. She might have done just that. But the smell of coffee drifted to her.

"Hey, sleepyhead." Sitting on the edge of the bed, Matt smiled as she jerked up.

"You're still here?"

His smile widened. What was obvious to him was that she'd thought he'd left. "Was I suppose to leave?" he asked while he set a breakfast tray on her bedside table.

"No." Taylor pushed herself to a sitting position with the gathered sheet to her breasts. She coiled her other arm around his neck, reveling in the warmth and texture of his skin beneath her fingers. Damp from a shower, his dark hair shone with red highlights.

Matt looked up from pouring her a cup of coffee. "You're beautiful." Unable to resist, he set the silver pot down first, then drew her into his arms. How much he needed her sweetness amazed him. As her mouth played over his, he released a muffled laugh against her lips. "If that's my reward for bringing you breakfast in bed, I'll do it every day."

More than anything, she wanted to hold him to words that hinted at a more-lasting relationship. With a sense of contentment that she hadn't believed could exist, she brushed her cheek against his.

Matt had awakened to the faint blush of dawn. With an arm draped across Taylor's waist and a leg tangled with hers, he'd listened to her slow, even breaths. At some moment during the night, in the darkness, she'd led him from the living room to the bedroom. Hell, he didn't remember when. He'd been in another world.

But reality bore down on him when he'd stood in the kitchen making coffee. He'd wondered then if they could separate love and passion, if they could share one without the other and not get hurt.

Seeing the faint frown line between his brows, Taylor wanted to beg him to just feel, stop thinking. Last night had been more than anything she'd ever imagined. "Last night was—"

"Perfect," he finished for her on a soft laugh.

"Yes, perfect." Her eyes closed, she breathed deeply to let the clean, masculine scent of him fill her mind.

As she shifted beside him, he curled his fingers over her thigh. "Don't you want any coffee?"

Not his question but a memory of last night snapped her eyes open. Angling a look at him, she frowned. "We left a mess in Lottie's kitchen."

Drawing back, Matt grinned at the worried look bunching her brows. "It's your kitchen."

"No, it's her kitchen." She shrugged in response to his amused grin. "Believe me, it's hers."

"I'll clean it up before I go outside." He dropped to his back beside her. In jeans, bare to the waist, he stretched out and crossed sock-clad feet at the ankles. Sunlight warmed the rich mahogany finish of the high-priced, antique furniture in the room. House beautiful, Matt thought. Nothing was out of place in the practically all-white bedroom. It was a blatant reminder of how different his place was, a reminder that he didn't have the right background, the right credentials for her. Alisha's father had said it bluntly. "You're not good enough."

"I've always let the kitchen belong to her," Taylor said as an explanation.

Matt brought his thoughts back to her. "Have you ever washed a dish in your life?"

Taylor looked askance at him with narrowed eyes. "Of course I have."

He chuckled at her indignant tone. "You haven't, have you?" He felt the shrug of her shoulder against his upper arm. In fairness, he knew there were things she'd done that he hadn't. "I've never gone to the opera," he told her.

His words surprised her. "Really, you haven't? I would have thought you might have when—"

As her voice trailed off, Matt guessed what she'd left unsaid. "When I was seeing Alisha?" He didn't wait for an answer. "Nope. Never went."

The conversation reminded her of an upcoming evening at a fund-raiser, one she'd promised Sarah she'd attend. "You still have a tuxedo, don't you?"

As she inched closer, turning on her side toward him, Matt grinned. "Is there something you want?"

A slow-forming smile curving her lips, she poked a finger at his bare chest. "Do you still own a tuxedo?"

Laughing, Matt caught her upper arms and brought her on top of him. "I get the feeling I don't want to admit that I do."

"Do you?" Taylor raised up to brace over him. Lightly she ran one finger in a slow circle down his belly.

He released a low-in-the-throat chuckle. "Unfair."

"What is?" she asked innocently.

"You know." Matt drew a quick breath as her hand dipped lower.

"Do you?"

An admittance meant a night in a monkey suit, he guessed. "Yeah. I own one," he said, because any thought of refusing her was futile with her mouth so near his again.

Chapter Nine

A routine began. Before eight every morning, Matt arrived to work on the garage. When Petey came home from school, he would stop and they'd spend time together. Taylor, too, had adjusted her life, cutting back her hours at the office to be home when Petey returned from school.

As a threesome they took long drives, enjoyed a picnic on the nearby mountains with the view of the sprawling city, rode bikes, played baseball, hiked and sometimes just sat and read a book to Petey or watched a video.

Alone with her, Matt romanced her. He brought flowers, called at midnight, saying he just wanted to hear her voice, and yesterday morning he arrived with bagels and cream cheese and fresh strawberries for breakfast.

Sipping coffee at the kitchen table, she knew she should have been content. Everything seemed so perfect. When in his arms, she felt wonderful, believed nothing could go wrong. But when away from him, she remembered his words about no promises. And that meant she had a problem because she'd changed her mind. She wanted everything he didn't want. Love, promises, marriage. All of it.

The click of the door opening scattered more such thoughts. Taylor looked up as Matt entered from outside. His hair tousled from the wind, he smiled at her in a slow teasing way she was becoming familiar with.

"Is this the real you?"

Taylor frowned. "The real...? Oh, my gosh," she said when his eyes sliced to her hair. Self-consciously she touched one of the rollers above her forehead.

"I'm going to lose all my mystery."

His laughter rippled out. "Mystery?"

"You know." She'd been missing him this morning, she realized in that instant. Eager to feel his arms around her, she stood as he stepped near. "One of those unknowns that keeps a man wondering."

He slid his arms around her waist. He thought she looked adorable in the blue silk kimono, fuzzy blue slippers and those jumbo pink rollers. "Give me an example. Is it something like wondering if her hair always looks so good?"

Taylor groaned. "Let's forget we ever started this."

Idly he fingered one of the rollers. He'd been so damn tired earlier, then he'd walked into the house.

The sight of her smile had drained away fatigue. "Can they come out?" he asked about the rollers, but was already slipping a pin from one. As hair tumbled out, he pleasurably toyed with the soft strands. "I love the feel of your hair." He chuckled against it. "I love the feel of you."

Lazily she let her lips roam the line of his strong jaw. She'd been yearning for the clean, soapy scent of him, for the feel of the iron hardness of his back beneath her fingertips. "You were gone for a while this morning, weren't you?" She'd looked out her bedroom window and hadn't seen his truck.

"I took Petey to school." Tenderness filling him, he bent his head and nuzzled the spot at the side of her neck that had caught his attention. "He's been hinting that he'd like to go to school in my truck. So I drove him."

Simple as that. As a child, she'd never known such sensitivity to her wants or desires. She'd received toys that her parents had thought were suitable. The one doll she'd longed for hadn't been bought because it was too ugly by her mother's standards. She'd received whatever any person could want, but no one had ever cared if it was what she wanted. "You are so special."

Easing back the opening of the robe, Matt sloughed off the compliment with a tease. "About time you noticed. Where's Lottie?"

Pleasurably she stroked his jaw and the stubble of his beard. "Coming in late." He could pretend he'd done nothing, but his thoughtfulness, his caring had drawn her to him from the beginning. "Would you like something to eat?"

"What are you offering?" He heard her moan when he nibbled at her earlobe.

"Something delicious," she managed to say.

He couldn't seem to get enough of her, he realized. "I've found it."

She nearly closed her eyes. Nearly. She heard the distinct chugging sound of Lottie's eight-year-old station wagon and released a whispery laugh. "Lottie's here. Don't forget where you were."

"Never." Matt drew back just as the door was opening.

With a bag of groceries cradled in her arm, Lottie lumbered in. She was inside and setting the bag on the kitchen counter before she noticed them. A rush of color brightened her round cheeks. "Excuse me, miss."

In passing, Matt touched her shoulder and winked, "I'm leaving, Lottie." He paused near the door, looking down in response to the sound of his beeper.

Taylor saw his frown as he read the caller's number. "Do you want to use the phone?" she asked, hoping he'd tell her if something was wrong.

"Nope. Don't know her."

Curiosity led her. "Should I be jealous?"

Matt could have told her that he'd thought of no other woman since he'd met her. "Lady, you have my heart."

Taylor wasn't sure who was more astonished by his words, but she saw regret flash in his eyes before he left her. He didn't want to care about her, not because she'd done something wrong, but because another woman had. It didn't matter. She wasn't going to let him take back those words.

With Petey at school and no appointments at the office, she treated herself to a morning at the salon. Feeling utterly feminine after a facial, manicure and pedicure, she returned home in a good mood, then dressed for afternoon tea with her aunt.

The hotel's dining room was done in a trendy, Southwestern, salmon and turquoise decor. The room buzzed with feminine voices, including her aunt's. She'd been talking in a soft tone about Ian for the past few moments. "He's becoming impatient, Taylor," she said while stirring a spoon in a slow, circular motion through her tea.

Taylor fiddled with the salmon-colored napkin. Marriage with him would never happen, she knew now. "I'm not going to marry him. I don't love him."

Her aunt went still. "I see," she said crisply.

"Aunt Maddie, I don't believe he would be good for Petey, either."

"This is about that man, isn't it?"

Taylor didn't doubt her aunt must have caught wind of the same gossip Sarah had mentioned.

"There's been talk about you and Mr. Duran. You're seeing him?"

"Yes, I am."

"Oh, dear." Instead of disapproval, concern clouded her eyes. "Taylor, this Mr. Duran makes a habit of pursuing young, rich women. First Alisha Marscroft and now you. Don't be taken in by him. If he's showing interest in you, you should question his need for money. Always examine a man's motives.''

Taylor believed her advice was well meant. ''Why do you assume he has to be interested in my money?''

''I didn't intend to hurt your feelings,'' her aunt was quick to say.

Taylor offered a smile. ''I know that.''

''Then—''

''Aunt Maddie, should I question Ian's reasons, too, for wanting to be with me?''

''Don't be ridiculous. His mother belonged to Daughters of the American Revolution. His father's a twenty-fifth cousin to royalty.'' Worry laced her voice. ''But this man—how do you know this man doesn't want your money?''

''I'll be careful,'' she said, hoping that promise ended the discussion.

Her aunt sighed resignedly. ''I believe that would be wise.''

But, of course, wisdom wasn't leading her. Her heart had opened to Matt. She refrained from telling her aunt that her advice had come too late. She was already in love.

Before heading to Petey's school to pick him up, she breezed into her favorite boutique and purchased a one-shoulder, black silk dress for the fund-raiser.

What to wear Wednesday evening bothered her more. Two days ago Matt had invited her and Petey to a nephew's birthday party. Nothing permanent, no commitment, Matt had said, but everything between them was changing. Was he realizing they could grab a second chance at happiness? Why else would he bother to take her and Petey to a family gathering?

Caught in traffic, she inched toward the corner. Seconds stretched to minutes before she negotiated a right-hand turn. Late because of shopping, she sped to Petey's school. He turned glum with her reminder about a dentist appointment.

An hour later, he remained downhearted. "I brush my teeth," he said as a protest to the hygienist's comments that plaque was gaining a stronghold. "Do you think I'll have to have braces?"

Taylor heard anxiety in his voice. "I had them."

"You did?"

She flashed a smile of white, even teeth at him. "It wasn't so bad. In fact, practically everybody in my class had them."

"They did?"

To stop his distress, she thought he needed a reminder. "That will be a long time from now. Let's forget about it."

Looking up at her, he nodded as if he thought that was a good idea. "Can I show Matt my new baseball cards?" he asked about the ones he'd gotten in a trade with a friend yesterday. "He said I could come see him anytime. Could we stop at his apartment?"

Taylor braked at a red light and glanced his way. "He might not be home."

"But he might be."

His optimism amazed her. How could she resist? Negotiating the car into the alley behind Matt's shop, she mused how his bright spirit more than anyone or anything had helped him recover after his parents' death.

"See, he's home," Petey said excitedly, breaking into her thoughts.

With a neighbor, Matt was carrying an armoire from the bed of a pickup truck toward his shop. While backing up toward the steel door, he spotted Taylor's car. In that instant he acknowledged that he'd felt something missing since he'd left her. A bond, a link existed with her and the boy. When he wasn't with them, he found himself thinking about them, wishing they were near. When he was alone, he told himself that he could walk away without hesitation. But when they were together, he knew that was a lie. "Hi, champ," he said when Petey jumped from the car and ran to him.

Taylor saw his smile in her direction. "Hi."

Matt continued to grin at her. "You got my message?"

She and Petey trailed them in to the shop. "What message?"

"I called."

Beside him now, Petey paced himself to Matt's stride. As if Matt had silently signaled him, he took the baseball cards out of his jeans pocket. "I got new baseball cards."

"I always liked baseball cards," the man with Matt piped in.

"These are some really bad ones," Petey assured both men.

"Thanks, Al," Matt said to the man.

"Anytime."

"So can I show the cards to you, Matt?"

Bracing his backside against the edge of his workbench, Matt kept his eyes on Taylor. With enjoyment, he watched her smile grow. "Why don't you lay them out on the desk." Over Petey's bent head, he mouthed, "I missed you."

That was all the encouragement Taylor needed. As Petey wandered into the apartment with his cards, she closed the distance to Matt. "Why did you call?"

He slipped his arms around her waist. "You already know."

She caught the gleam of amusement in his eyes and laughed. With a fingertip, she traced the faint smile line bracketing a corner of his mouth. "Tell me."

"I called to tell you that I missed you." Gently he nibbled at her top lip. "Want to stay? I'll make tacos."

A laugh rose in her throat. "How could I refuse?"

At the shrill of the phone behind him, Matt slid a hand down her hip to hold her close. "Ignore it."

As much as she wanted to, his suggestion proved impossible. While the phone rang behind him, someone rapped on the door behind her.

Laughter crept into his voice. "I don't believe this."

"You're in demand," she said and smiled at his scowl of displeasure as much as the situation.

"Seems so," he grumbled, giving her a quick kiss before turning toward the phone.

Finding the situation humorous, she whirled around. "Just a minute," she called in response to a more demanding knock on the door. But before she reached it, it swung open. The sight of Matt's sister instantly sent a rush of uneasiness through her. Last time they'd met, Cara had made it clear that she didn't like her.

For a long, uncomfortable moment, they stood in silence staring at each other.

"I'm sorry about before," Cara said when Taylor made a move to walk away. She gave Taylor a sheepish look. "And I'm sorry about this. I...I keep barging in at the wrong moment, don't I?"

Her smile meant more to Taylor than her words. Though she didn't understand why, Taylor sensed the effort being made for a friendliness that had been lacking the last time they'd met. "Matt's on the phone." Awkward about what to do, Taylor wandered toward Petey.

"We got off on the wrong foot last time," Cara said behind her.

Taylor stilled. Wrong foot? She'd made it clear she didn't like her.

"I didn't want you to hurt him," she said as an explanation. "Well, I mean that I thought you would hurt him."

Taylor faced her. Since that meeting, Matt had shared more of his past with her. How could she fault his sister for loving her brother, wanting to protect him? "You don't have to explain," she said to ease Cara's discomfort.

"He was hurt so badly by Alisha."

"I know," Taylor said. "She walked out on him when he lost his money."

"Yes, but—" Confusion sharpened Cara's expressive eyes. "Is that all he told you?"

Before Taylor had a chance to respond, Matt appeared in the kitchen doorway.

"Hi. What's up?" he asked, ambling toward them. He noticed there was no tension in the air between them like before.

For his benefit, because she sensed how much he wanted them to like each other, Taylor brought forth a smile despite troubled thoughts. She couldn't help wondering what Cara had meant. Had something happened between Alisha and him that he hadn't shared with her, didn't trust her enough to know?

"Did you get the message?" Cara was asking Matt.

"Depends on what message you're talking about." He moved toward Petey, who was standing by the desk and spreading his baseball cards on it. As he scanned the baseball cards, he touched the boy's shoulder.

"The message from Expressions Gallery."

"Someone from there left a message on my beeper," Matt said distractedly, noting Petey had gotten a rookie card of an old-time catcher. "How she got it—"

"I gave her your beeper number," Cara broke in.

Over his shoulder, he scowled at her. "Thanks a lot. That's a good card," he said to Petey as he pointed at one.

"So might this be," Cara said in a tone that said pay attention. "Here." She handed him a business card. "Lannie Esten. Remember the name? She wants to do a show."

"Of what?"

"Of your carvings." She rolled her eyes, looking toward Taylor. "He's not usually so dense."

From her shoulder bag, Cara took out a notepad. "I wrote down her words. She said, 'The art community needs new blood, new artists.' She wants you to bring over some of your pieces."

Matt refused to gape. Was she really saying what he'd thought he heard? Few galleries were interested in taking chances on unknowns. They showed only the works of "name" artists. He looked up to see his sister at the door.

"I'm out of here."

Matt laughed at her speedy exit and fingered the card. An artist? He couldn't believe she'd called him that. He mulled over the idea of collecting big money for doing something he loved. Sounded too perfect.

"Call me," Cara said before closing the door behind her.

Turned away, Taylor dealt with her troubled thoughts. If his lack of trust hurt her, that was her own fault. "This is wonderful, Matt," she said, facing him, truly pleased about what was happening to him. When she'd seen his carvings that day weeks ago, she'd been impressed by the originality, the skill in his intricately detailed sculptures.

As much as Matt wanted to run with the excitement, jumping to conclusions wasn't his way. He planned to keep a tight rein on emotion until he talked to the woman. "She just wants to talk."

"You could be famous."

"Or a starving artist because no one will buy any of it."

His response made her smile. If she'd been asked to describe him, she'd have said he was pragmatic, sensible, down-to-earth. Leaning toward him, she curled an arm around his neck. "Are you fishing for compliments?"

Matt tossed out a tease. "If you cared, you'd say the right lines."

She grabbed at the lighthearted moment. "Like, 'Of course, they'll buy your pieces, Matt.'" She gushed, "'They're wonderful.'"

He kissed her nose. "She's picking on me," he said to Petey who was smiling, enjoying the scene before him.

"*I* didn't," he quickly reminded Matt.

Matt crossed to him and draped an arm around his shoulders. "That's because you're my pal."

Petey beamed. "Can we stay while you're gone, Matt?" he asked, indicating he'd been paying attention to the conversation. "We could play with the train, couldn't we?"

Like him, Taylor wasn't ready to leave. If they stayed, they'd be able to share in his good news when he came back. "If it's okay, we'll wait."

In passing, he brushed his knuckles across her cheek. "Okay. I'll be back as soon as I can."

When the door closed behind him, Petey ran to the window to watch him drive away. "Matt's happy, isn't he?"

Back in the kitchen, Taylor opened one cupboard and then another in her search for a coffee cup. "Yes, he got good news," she said, feeling pleased as she located blue mugs.

"Shouldn't we make a cake then?"

Frowning, Taylor pivoted toward him.

His brows bunched as if he were suddenly unsure about his suggestion. "When Daddy got a new job, Mommy made one."

"And you had a party?"

"Uh-huh."

Little by little, he was teaching her about a life she'd never known. "Okay, then." She stretched across the counter to reach Matt's phone. "I'll call Lottie to make one."

"No, we should make it, Aunt Taylor." She watched his frown deepen. "You know how, don't you?"

Anyone could bake a cake, she assured herself. "Of course."

Matt wondered if he was flying. A few weeks ago he'd been just going along. He would get up, go to work, come home. He'd occasionally gone out on a date. Suddenly his life had taken a turn. A woman and child had come into his life. He'd begun to think about the future again. And now an excitement he hadn't felt since he was a kid accompanied him as he returned home.

When he opened the back door, the smell of something freshly baked drifted to him. For the past four years he'd lived in the small apartment behind his shop and not once had it smelled so good. Christmastime of his youth and homemade cookies came to mind.

He wandered through his weight room to the kitchen. It was a mess. But he gave the sinkful of dirty bowls only a glance.

Beaming, Petey held a plate bearing a lopsided chocolate cake. "We made it."

And wore it, Matt thought, amused, maintaining a deadpan expression at the dab of chocolate frosting on Taylor's cheek. By the smear around Petey's mouth, he surmised the boy had sampled it. "A cake?"

"For you." Petey sort of grimaced. "It'll be good now. We picked the egg shells out of the bowl. Well, some might still be in the cake."

For him. They'd done this for him. "Why did you do this?"

Taylor saw incredulity in his eyes. How could he not know that they loved him? That they wanted it all with him. "It was Petey's idea. For a celebration. You do have good news, don't you?"

"Yeah." He couldn't help smiling. "She wants to do a show of my work."

"Matt, that's wonderful." She rushed into his arms.

With her hug, Petey flew at his legs, not wanting to be left out.

Emotion swelling within him, he felt a tightness in his chest. As he gathered them both close, he drew a hard breath. He hadn't expected their joy on his behalf. He hadn't expected to feel so pleased. Damn, say it like it is. They made him feel important—loved. They made him want it all again, he realized.

The cake tasted great. Matt didn't care if the texture was a little nutty. Eggshells wouldn't kill him. Afterward they went to a movie, a double feature that included an animated version of *Tarzan.*

As they inched their way along with the crowd exiting the theater, Matt linked his hand with Taylor's. Walking beside them, Petey yawned and began to drag his feet with tiredness. ''I don't remember where you parked,'' he said when they neared the parking lot with its rows of cars.

Hearing the fatigue in his voice, Matt halted and turned to pick him up. ''Over there.'' Anticipating that Petey might be tired before they got home, Matt had driven Taylor's car instead of his truck, so the boy would be more comfortable.

''In the apple section?'' he asked on another yawn, curling a slim arm around Matt's neck.

''Orange,'' Matt answered. He squeezed Taylor's hand. ''Why so quiet?''

For the past few moments, her mind had wandered with the realization of how much fuller her life was now. Her friends didn't know the joy of accomplishment from baking a cake, the youthful ridiculousness that she'd experienced while playing imaginary games with Petey, the fulfillment of watching a little boy's face grow wide with a grin because he'd mastered something new and challenging. And had any of her friends ever felt the encompassing passion for a man like she felt for Matt?

"Taylor?"

She gave him a quick grin. "I'm sorry." How could she tell him of the longing in her heart for his love? "I was thinking about the fund-raiser," she said instead, because she'd meant to discuss it with him earlier. "When you pick me up, could you come half an hour earlier? I promised Sarah I'd be there early."

Matt didn't want to go. The thought had hit him days ago. If he went, wouldn't he have gone full circle? How many fund-raisers had he attended with Alisha? How many nights of inconsequential conversation with people he never saw again had he endured? Turning away, he unlocked Taylor's car. "Listen, Taylor." He started and stopped, knowing she wasn't going to be happy about what he would say.

She didn't like sentences that started that way.

"Would you believe me if I said I can't find my tux?"

The tenseness in his voice didn't slip past her. He'd spoken lightly, but he was dead serious. "You said you'd go with me. If you can't find one, couldn't you rent one?"

Matt stepped back, opened the door and eased a sleepy Petey into the car. "So you're not buying my excuse of a lost tux?"

"If you really don't want to go—" She paused. If she took his words too seriously, the moment might get out of hand. "I suppose I could get someone else to take me," she said with a levity she didn't feel.

Bent over Petey in the back seat, Matt buckled a seat belt around him. Hell, that wouldn't do, either. He didn't want to go. But he didn't want her with some other guy, either. Straightening beside her, he planned to argue, then he saw her impish smile. "Not nice."

"What is this really all about?" she asked more seriously now that he no longer looked so uptight.

Truthfulness made sense to Matt. "I went to enough of those."

"You went to them with another woman," she reminded him. If he was trying to distance himself, she refused to let him. "Not with me."

A sliver of a moon peeked out from behind quick-moving clouds, only to hide again. Beneath the lights in the parking garage, her eyes appeared darker, almost fathomless. "No, not with you," he said softly. With the heat of her breath warming his face, he pulled her against him. What had started this? Insecurities from before? Because too many emotions were too close to the surface, he chose the easiest way. "I'll go." A longing stirred inside him to ease away the troubled line marring her forehead. "Forget it."

Taylor was wise enough to know they'd only postponed a similar tension-filled conversation. For now, though, she followed his lead. While she was in his embrace, she wouldn't let herself think about where they would go from here. Being with him, like this, was all that mattered.

Chapter Ten

Matt had disciplined himself to work out in his weight room every morning. To the sound of Garth Brooks's latest hit, he counted off the last of the arm curls, then snatched a towel from the bench press. Wiping the towel over his sweaty face, he wandered into the bathroom to shower.

Unknowingly Taylor was forcing him to face a lot more than he wanted to. Repeatedly he'd dodged labeling what he felt for her. Sure he cared about her, about her and Petey. But love? Did he dare believe in it again?

When he arrived at her house later, he saw her aunt's limousine parked in front, as if to mock him for considering love with the daughter of J. Harrington Elmhurst. Whenever he spent time alone with Taylor, nothing else mattered. The problem was they weren't always alone. No one lived in a vacuum. She had her share of highbrow relatives and acquaintances. Regardless of what they might feel, he believed her social standing and wealth were wedged firmly between them as a reminder of how different her life was from his.

With effort, he knuckled down to his work. Keeping his mind on it wasn't easy. On a grassy knoll near the flower garden, Taylor and Petey played catch until it began to rain, coming down in huge drops. Then they ran into the house.

As lightning flashed in the distance a few minutes later, Matt shut off his saw. He could fool himself into believing he had a taste for Lottie's lemonade, or an addiction for her cookies. None of that was true. He dashed toward the back door of the house, aware he simply wanted to be with them.

At the kitchen door he stopped instead of opening it. Seated beside Petey at the kitchen table, her blond head close to his, Taylor was running her paint-coated fingertips beside his over a paper. From a distance, the drawing looked like an abstract. He assumed it didn't matter what it looked like. Seeing their smiles, hearing their laughter, Matt backed off. With the rain pouring down on him, he wandered back to the garage. It was a moment for the two of them, a chance to bond; they didn't need him barging in.

She really had changed, he acknowledged. She'd become more than a guardian to the boy. As Matt had suspected weeks ago, she hadn't needed someone to help her. She'd just needed to let love grow between her and the boy. And he had to face a more painful realization. The woman who'd asked for his help really didn't need it anymore.

Fun. Taylor couldn't recall ever doing something so silly or having so much fun. Even as a child, she'd never been allowed such ridiculousness as finger-painting. Why was obvious. Messiness hadn't been a word in her mother's vocabulary.

In the bathroom, she scrubbed at her nails. A hint of green outlined several of them. Short on time, she forgot any notion of a manicure before she went to the office. She repaired her nails as best she could, then dressed in a long navy dress with white flowers and her dark pumps.

Stuck in traffic later, she concentrated on the cars ahead of her and impatiently tapped a finger at her steering wheel. Windshield wipers swished. Behind her, someone honked. She hit the switch on her CD. The lulling notes of "Moonlight Sonata" filled the inside of the car as traffic finally inched forward.

Despite the traffic jam, she made good time, arriving with a few minutes to spare before her meeting with Martin. During the elevator ride up, she mentally debated about which dress to wear to tonight's gathering for Matt's nephew's birthday party. She wanted his family to like her. Without doing anything, she'd been out of favor with Cara when they'd first met simply because she was Taylor Elmhurst. What if the rest of his relatives felt the same way?

Stop it, she berated herself. If she didn't, she'd drive herself crazy with worries that might not even exist. Matt wouldn't have invited her and Petey if he thought they wouldn't have a good time. She'd learned that about him. He possessed some wonderful traits, especially sensitivity and consideration for others' feelings. They would have a good time, she convinced herself by the time elevator doors swooshed open.

In her office, lack of sunlight chilled the room. Thick gray clouds hid the tops of skyscrapers. Thunder rumbled. Rain drummed against the window at a steady beat. She smiled a thank-you when her assistant brought in the mail and a cup of coffee.

Settled behind her desk, she sorted through her opened mail, pausing to read an inspector's report about one of the apartment complexes. When the door opened, she looked up, expecting to see Martin.

Instead of him, Ian stood in the doorway, a not-too-convincing smile curved the edges of his lips. "I've missed you. Every time I call, you're out," he said as he neared the desk. "So I've come to take you to lunch."

She'd been schooled to keep her emotions suppressed. Her mother had preached that an Elmhurst didn't raise her voice in public. "I wished you'd called." She made much about nudging back the cuff of her blouse to check her watch, even though a digital clock was on her desk. "I don't plan to be here that long. I have a meeting, and then I want to arrive back home to have lunch with Petey when he gets home from school."

His smile looked even more forced suddenly. "Your concern for him is admirable, darling, but you have your own life to lead.'' He sat on the edge of her desk. ''A lunch away from him wouldn't hurt.''

''You don't understand.'' Edgy, looking for something to do with her hands, Taylor reached for a manila file folder. ''I want to be there for him.''

''Is this some maternal phase you're going through?''

Straightening her back, she took a long, slow breath to keep her temper at bay. ''I'm not *playing* mother. And anything I do with Petey comes first before everything else.''

''You sound like the lioness protecting her cub.''

She realized he truly believed she wasn't capable of such maternal feelings. At one time she might have agreed with him. Selfish, self-centered women made poor mothers. But that Taylor had changed. She no longer awakened with only thoughts of herself. ''I'm busy today,'' she said, instead of bothering to defend her actions. What he thought didn't matter.

''Dinner then,'' he insisted.

''I can't.'' Here goes, she realized. ''I have a date.''

His eyes darkened with irritation. ''So, it's true.''

Taylor stared at him. ''Pardon?''

''There's been talk about you and the carpenter.''

''Ian, I've been honest with you. I'm not going to marry you.''

''Taylor, what's come over you?'' He released a soft mirthless laugh. ''We belong together. Marriage between us would be beneficial. I'm sure your aunt has discussed this with you.''

"You make it sound more like a merger than a marriage."

"That is ridiculous," he said, looking affronted. "Who in the world has been filling your mind with such nonsense?"

No one but him. Thoughtfully she studied him. He sounded more than annoyed.

"If you'd think clearly about us, you'd see that marrying me is the right thing to do. Why are you suddenly so sure that I'm wrong for you? Because of that carpenter?" In an unnatural movement, he raked a hand through his perfectly combed hair, messing it. "If your father was here none of this would happen." Exasperation edged his voice. "He always investigated the men you dated. Without him around, you need me."

Taylor sent him a disbelieving look that passed by unnoticed. There was a desperateness in his voice. Why? She searched his eyes for what wasn't visible. Why so much urgency? "No, *you* need me, don't you?"

His chin jerked up as if he'd been punched.

"This isn't about love. It's about money." She'd been guessing, but he looked as guilty as a child caught with his hand in the cookie jar. Money never stopped being a part of every phase of her life, she realized. "What have you done, Ian? Why do you need me so badly?"

Matt noted her quietness, her strained smile when he picked her and Petey up that evening. He fought his own uncertainties and said nothing. But he couldn't help wondering if she was feeling forced to go with him out of politeness. She'd accepted the invitation to his parents' home, but with time to think, was she regretting that quick decision? This wasn't the usual kind of event on her social calendar.

He braked in front of a ranch-style home where cars were parked on the driveway and on both sides of the street. Matt would bet that the adult Taylor had never been to a kid's birthday party. She'd told him she'd begun seeing her brother only recently, which made Matt wonder if she'd missed most of Petey's birthday parties.

"There are a lot of people here," she said.

Matt peered at her in the darkness inside her car. "Are you okay with this?"

"Okay?" She smiled as she became aware of what he meant. "Absolutely. I'm just nervous." She wasn't lying.

"Don't be."

"Easier said than done," she responded. She pressed a hand to her nervous stomach before she slid out of the car. She waited with Petey for Matt to round the front and join them.

It would have been easy to have accepted what she'd told him and said no more, but he'd been around her often enough to sense her tension. "Why don't you tell me what's wrong?"

"Can I go ahead?" Petey interrupted. He'd been anticipating the day ever since Taylor told him about it. When she'd returned from the office, he'd been full of questions. How many kids would be there?

Would there be cake and ice cream? What if they don't like him?

It had been easy for Taylor to reassure him that he shouldn't worry about that. They would like him. She wished she could have said the same thing about herself with such certainty. "Only to the door," she said, knowing without that stipulation he would walk in on his own. Shy, he wasn't.

To get her attention, Matt laid a hesitant hand on her shoulder. "There's more wrong, isn't there?"

A ghost of a smile touched her eyes. She hadn't meant to spoil the day, but while Matt was driving, she'd had time to think, to remember the scene in her office. "I saw Ian today. He made me realize who I am."

"Matt," Petey called impatiently.

Taylor touched Matt's arm. "Can we talk later?"

Wanting, no, needing to see her eyes, he cupped her chin. "This is about Ian?"

Shadows emphasized the hard angles and the hollows in his face. Taylor tightened her grip on his hand. "I'm sorry if I—"

"Never mind," Matt said quickly. He bent forward and pressed his mouth to hers. He'd been acting like an idiot. Unlike Alisha, she didn't wear a false face. She truly believed in what they were sharing.

More nervous than she'd ever been in her life, Taylor had enough to think about. Butterflies took flight in her stomach when he opened the door.

"We're here," Matt yelled.

Letting Petey precede her in the house, she froze

at the door, stunned at the number of people crammed inside. "There are so many."

Matt offered an understanding grin and kissed the shell of her ear. "Neighbors and friends." He slipped an arm around her waist. "Come on. I'll introduce you to everyone."

"Beginning with me."

Taylor returned the warm smile of a broad-shouldered man with salt-and-pepper hair and thick, horn-rimmed glasses.

"My father," Matt told her.

The handshake he offered was firm, warm. "It's nice you could come. You, too," he said to Petey before a laughing, dark-haired girl around Petey's age ran up to him with a question.

"My niece," Matt told Taylor after they'd moved away. "And the kid with a leg draped over the arm of the chair and the hair that's longer than yours is my nephew—Josh."

"He's sixteen. He's seeking his own identity," a feminine voice behind them said as an excuse, then offered her hand to Taylor. "I'm Moira Duran. We're happy you both could come."

Taylor felt none of her previous apprehension. "Thank you."

Matt's mother was a petite woman with a quick smile and pure white hair. "You weren't easy to put up with at that age," she teased Matt.

"I wasn't?" Grinning, he draped an arm around her shoulder. "You're kidding. You mean I wasn't the perfect son?"

"Oh, yes." She winked at Taylor. "He was perfect."

Matt chuckled at that.

Smiling, his mother resumed the role of hostess. "There's plenty of food." She spoke softer as she turned her attention to Petey who'd been clinging close to Taylor's side. "You're Petey, aren't you? Did you bring a big appetite?"

"Uh-huh," he said, nodding.

"That's good. Because we have lots of food. If you like to play video games, that's what my grandchildren are doing. Would you like to meet them?"

Petey looked up at Taylor, waiting for her okay.

"If you'd like to, go ahead," Taylor said.

Moira offered him a hand. "Come on."

Already eyeing the game, Petey went with her. Over his shoulder, he flashed a smile at Taylor. She assumed his anxiety about being liked by Matt's family had faded.

As they moved away, a man sidled close and clamped a hand over Matt's shoulder. "So you got here." Though a few inches shorter and a few pounds heavier than Matt, he had the same firm jaw, high cheekbones and quick smile as Matt. "He's notoriously late to everything," he said to Taylor.

Matt offered his brother an affectionate and good-natured grin. "This is Tom."

"Don't forget me," a feminine voice piped in.

"And his wife, Renee," Matt said on a laugh.

Matt's sister-in-law was warm and welcoming, a youthful-looking brunette with flashing dark eyes. She stayed a moment, then left to supervise her three children, the sixteen-year-old whose eyes were riveted to the basketball game on the television set, an eleven-year-old who was the birthday boy, and the little one who'd left her grandpa to show Petey the video game.

Dinner played out noisily, conversation punctuated by laughter. Taylor learned that Matt's dad had had a stroke, but had worked his way through rehabilitation. After his health improved, he and Matt's mother had joined Matt and Cara in Arizona. Months later, Tom and his family had followed.

Sitting with Matt on a bay window seat, Taylor checked on Petey. On the floor, he giggled at the antics of Matt's young niece. Nearby, looking unruffled, Matt's mother was returning from the kitchen, a towel dangling from her hand. Along with Tom she mopped up a glass of spilled milk. "You have a great family," Taylor said, envious because he had what she'd only dreamed about.

Matt had wanted to see her among his family to convince himself that anything permanent between them wouldn't work. But she fit in perfectly.

"Your taste in women has improved," Tom said, having wandered back to them. "Remember Tracey?"

Within hearing range, Cara offered an explanation, "Tracey Hungens pierced everything."

Taylor smiled, sensing they were having fun at Matt's expense.

Behind Tom, his youngest bellowed her displeasure at a neighbor boy taking a potato chip from her plate. As he and Cara turned to play peacemakers, Taylor leaned her head close to Matt's. "Was Tracey your first love?"

Matt slanted a grin at her. "My first love was Ashley Bonmetter."

Interested, Taylor shifted on the seat toward him. "How old were you?"

Matt poked his fork into the mound of potato salad on his plate. "Five."

Taylor tried to visualize him at five, a boyish grin, devilment in his eyes. "She was in your kindergarten class?"

"The first day of school, I was convinced that I'd marry her or Julie Hoffenbaum."

"So two women had won your heart?"

"Until the second day. That's when Julie Hoffenbaum yelled at me." He chuckled, remembering he'd been heartbroken. "She was my teacher." Close by, Tom settled on the floor between his two younger kids. Matt was satisfied with his life, but his brother had one thing that he'd wanted for years, a family of his own. Fate sure threw curves, he realized. He could only play out a game of what-ifs with Taylor. What if she wasn't an Elmhurst came to mind first. He knew the answer. He'd have been reeling with certainty about a lifetime with her.

"What did you do wrong?" Taylor asked, bringing him back to the moment.

He gave her a crooked grin. "I yanked on Ashley's ponytail." He set his plate aside on an end table nearby. "She fell in love then. After the ponytail yank, I was her one and only." The memory broadened his grin. "So did you have a first love?" he asked.

"When I was twelve," she said between bites of a pickle, "I adored Andrew Phillips III."

By the name, he sounded like someone suitable for her.

Taylor sent him a breezy smile. "I was shy, gangly and wearing braces."

And a breath away from being the beauty she was today, Matt guessed. "And he was?"

"He was a much older man. All of fourteen, and so sophisticated." That drew his soft laugh. "Well, that's what we thought."

"Who's we?"

"Sarah and I. We were all in the same dance class."

During the past weeks, Matt had had more contact with the brunette. He'd liked her instantly, sensing an ability to laugh at herself when he'd seen the gleam of mischief in her eyes. From affectionate comments Taylor had made about Sarah, he assumed they were as close as sisters. "And was he taken with you?"

"He didn't know I existed. By the time he noticed me years later, I wanted no part of him." With a napkin, she wiped her fingers of pickle juice. "He had a reputation for being a narcissistic bore."

"Aunt Taylor," Petey interrupted, squeezing into the space between her and Matt. "You should see the game with the tennis players." Excitement raised his young voice. "It's really neat. When I get bigger can I take tennis lessons?"

Taylor smiled, recalling he'd seen a movie with a

fireman last week and had insisted he was going to be one. The week before that he'd wanted to be Superman. But while he might change his mind about the tennis lessons, that he'd asked her about them carried a lot of importance. It meant he was finally getting more comfortable with his new surroundings. Until that moment he hadn't talked about anything beyond the immediate future. "We'll see."

"Okay," he said easily, becoming distracted by Matt's nephew calling him.

Matt smirked at her when Petey stepped away. "'We'll see.' I always hated that response from my parents. It usually meant no."

She laughed and balled her napkin. "What did you ask for?"

Off the top of his head, Matt honestly couldn't recall anything.

"It was really important, wasn't it?" she teased.

He touched a strand of hair near her cheek. "At twelve, I thought so," he answered as a memory sprang forward. "I wanted certain sneakers. They had a designer's name on it. Hell, everything had a name on it. Kids wouldn't buy T-shirts or shorts or shoes unless they had certain names on them. Anyway when I asked for them, my parents said—"

"We'll see," she finished for him.

He laughed with her. "Yeah. But then a week went by, and I asked again. I told them that all the guys at school were wearing them. That argument never went over very big with my parents. They always came back with the standard parent line."

He sparked her curiosity. "What was that?"

"If everyone was jumping off a building, would you do that, too?"

"I remember saying that," Matt's father piped in.

Matt stood and grinned at him. "You had a lot of words of wisdom. Do you want coffee, Taylor?"

For a chance to be alone with Matt's father and get to know him better, she would have agreed, even if she hadn't wanted the coffee.

Though his father started to take the seat that Matt had vacated, his wife calling his name kept him standing. "We'll have to talk later."

Taylor smiled her agreement.

"By the way." He touched her shoulder. "Matt's never brought a friend to a family party before."

Taylor assumed he meant a female and wondered why Matt had never brought Alisha to meet his parents. Her hope to learn more ended when Renee carried out a birthday cake.

Only later, after gifts were opened and Matt was busy helping put together one of his nephew's new toys, Cara provided her with information. "I overheard what my dad said to you. I know you're wondering why Matt's been so selective in who he brings for us to meet." She gathered paper plates and napkins from the coffee table. "My meeting with Alisha wasn't pleasant. I knew what Matt felt for her and really wanted to meet her. I ran into them one day while shopping. After Matt introduced us, she turned away without even a nice-to-meet-you."

"She snubbed you?" With Cara's nod, Taylor understood better now why Matt's sister had been un-

friendly when they'd met. By association, because of
her wealth, she'd been linked to Alisha.

"You know Matt," Cara went on. "He wouldn't
deliberately hurt anyone. After that meeting, he told
me that he would never again be responsible for
bringing someone near any of us who might hurt us
like that."

Those words gave Taylor a lot to think about. Did
bringing her to meet his family mean he did trust her?

"Where are you?" Matt asked against her ear.

Taylor noticed then that Cara had moved away. "I
was wishing you were near." In passion, he heated
her blood, but it was this gentleness she had no defense against. She turned in his arms to face him, saw
the gleam of humor in his eyes.

A grin tugged at his mouth. "I was wishing we
were alone."

Despite his words, it was past midnight when they
left for Taylor's home. Petey, sleeping on one of the
sofas in Matt's parents' living room, barely stirred
when Matt carried him to the car and then later from
the car to his bedroom.

Amusement and tenderness mingled within Matt as
he listened to Petey's soft, even breaths so close to
his ear. "He sleeps through anything, doesn't he," he
said rather than asked after he settled him on the train-
shaped bed.

Taylor pulled off one of Petey's sneakers and then
the other. "He fights going to sleep, but once he does,
nothing wakes him," she said while working off his
jeans.

Straightening, Matt noted Petey had hung a poster

of a basketball star they'd picked up days ago beside one of another sports figure. On an adjacent wall, his school artwork was tacked to a bulletin board. Scanning the room, he saw a blanket draped between a dresser and a small table. "What's that?"

"It's his tent." Taylor tossed Petey's socks into a hamper. "We built it the other morning." After her first cup of coffee, she'd been drawn into the game of hiding from imaginary dinosaurs.

Matt rounded a grin at her. "We?"

"We."

Matt gave her credit. "You're doing really well with him."

Taylor decided that was the nicest compliment he could have given her. "I made a change today at the office so I don't have to be there so much."

"I thought you had done that already," Matt responded in a whispery voice so he wouldn't wake Petey.

"I did, but now Martin will be doing more." Though she would still make the final decisions on financial issues, she'd delegated more responsibilities to Martin.

Matt caught her at the waist as they stepped into the hallway. The Taylor Elmhurst he'd first met hadn't understood that all one little boy had needed had been her time and her love. "Do you want company tonight?"

Taylor swayed into his embrace and pressed her cheek to his. Eyes half-closed, she heard the shrill of the telephone, but didn't move away.

Soft and almost condescending, Ian's voice played

on the answering machine. ''Taylor, I know it's late, but call me. We need to talk about this misunderstanding.''

Recalling her last conversation with him revived her feeling of annoyance.

Matt felt her stiffen before she started to draw back. Keeping a firm hold on her shoulders, he made her face him. ''Something happened?''

''Nothing that surprised me.'' Earlier she'd walked out on Ian. She'd heard enough to convince her that nothing he said would change one fact. ''He admitted that everything between us had been because he needed money.''

Concern rose within him. He wasn't certain what emotion she was dealing with. Disappointment, anger, heartache. What did she feel? ''Did he disappoint you because you cared about him?''

Taylor took the hand he offered and moved with him to the sofa. ''I never wanted to marry him,'' she said to clarify what her relationship had been with him before Matt had come into her life. ''But I cared about him. I thought he was a friend. I'm just…hurt, I guess, to learn someone else in my life had only one concern—money.''

Sitting and facing her, their knees almost touching, Matt saw the struggle within her. With a fingertip, he brushed back strands of her hair near her cheek. He knew her childhood, her past with another man. One night in the darkness of her room she'd told him about some guy named Justin who hadn't understood how special she was, hadn't treasured her. And now another person had hurt her.

"He told me he was in trouble. He needed money, a lot of it because of gambling debts." Taylor shrugged a shoulder, but the gray eyes on her wouldn't let her feign such indifference. "It's my own fault. I never checked his background. I've been told since I was old enough to date that I should always check a man's background."

Matt didn't ask her to confirm that she'd done just that with him. "And you didn't with Ian?"

"I wouldn't do that to a man I was seeing," she said pointedly, wanting him to understand that she knew only what he'd told her about himself. "My father always did it, though." He'd said she was too gullible, but she wanted to believe in people. "Ian admitted that his family has no money anymore. Their lineage is excellent—their assets aren't. So he needs to marry a rich woman." That seemed to be her biggest asset. She was a rich woman. Every man she'd ever met had noticed that first about her, wanted her because of it. She felt Matt's hand tightening on hers. Every man except this one, whose bitter memories with a woman of wealth shadowed them. How ironic that her money might be what would keep them apart.

Lightly Matt framed her face with his hands. "I'm sorry he let you down."

She shook her head, wanting to ban Ian's image and thoughts of him. As Matt's lips hovered above hers, she realized how much she needed to be in his arms. Coiling her arms around his neck, she shut her eyes.

When his mouth closed over hers, she sank against him. Her heart was his to break, she knew. Though he was a good man and wouldn't mean to, he could hurt her badly. But even as she knew she might not be with him forever, it was too late to pull back. To be with him now, to grab whatever happiness she could have, she was willing to take the risk.

Chapter Eleven

Thursday morning Taylor did volunteer work for the local animal shelter. The annual ''adoptathon'' had been successful, and she felt enormous satisfaction at being there.

Earlier she'd labored to get out of bed, to leave Matt's side. Snoring softly he'd mumbled something unintelligible when she'd eased from the arm she'd been using for a pillow. She'd watched him burrow deeper beneath the blanket, then she'd forced her feet to the floor.

Now, with a goodbye to other volunteers, she strolled to her car, eager to see him again. Walking ahead of her, a woman cooed with delight at the terrier she'd adopted. More good images made her feel wonderful as she returned home—the sweet face of a golden retriever, his long tongue lapping at his new owner's face; the tan kitten cuddled like a baby in the elderly woman's arms; the two-year-old German shepherd with worshiping eyes fixed on the nine-year-old boy who was petting it.

Smiling as she neared the house, she flicked off the music in her car. When she followed the final curve to the driveway, she spotted Matt and Petey near the garage playing basketball. Today was *the* big game. Since eight-thirty, Petey had been awake, Matt had told her when he'd called her on her cell phone at ten this morning. Aware of Petey's impatience level, she merely waved, then rushed to her room to change clothes.

While zipping her denim skirt, she heard the thumping of the basketball from outside. Spurts of laughter accompanied the sounds of Matt's and Petey's voices. She was convinced they all belonged together and believed that Matt eventually would admit that to himself. Already he treated Petey with such loving care he could have been his own, and she couldn't believe what they'd found wouldn't last. Time. All they needed was time together.

Her pace quick, she went down the hall and was stepping outside just as Petey was coming in to get her.

"Are you ready?"

"Why?" she teased. "Is something special happening today?"

He was dressed in a slightly oversize green-and-white-striped uniform with the number on the back of the shirt and a solid green cap. "It's my first game."

He touched the bill of the cap. Too big, it sat low on his ears. "Remember?"

"Oh, yes, that's right."

Amusement sparkled in his eyes. "You're teasing me, aren't you?"

She caught him to her and hugged him. "Just a little."

Barely able to contain his excitement, he chattered during the drive to the field. "We had show-and-tell at school yesterday. Know what happened?"

Matt took his cue. "What happened?" he asked, but over Petey's head, his gaze hung on Taylor. Sunlight bathed her a soft glow.

"Joey brought his guinea pig." He turned eyes dancing with delight up at Matt. "And it got out, and the girls were screaming, and Miss Janek got real red."

Matt would guess that had been the best moment of the day. He wheeled the truck into the parking lot near the field. He recalled a garden snake he'd found on the way to school that he'd let loose in the cafeteria. At nine years old he'd taken great delight in watching his homeroom teacher jump on a chair and screech.

When Matt parked, Petey unsnapped his seat belt. "The best was Christi's," he went on before following Taylor out of the truck. "She brought cupcakes. And after she showed them, we got to eat them. There's Jessica." He pointed at a little girl he went to school with who was on his team. "Can I go by her, Aunt Taylor?"

"Go ahead." As he took off, Taylor linked her

hand with Matt's. "How often did he ask what time it was?"

"Every five minutes." Matt steered her toward a bleacher. The hand in his was soft. Everywhere her skin was soft as velvet. As her shoulder brushed his arm when they squeezed past several people standing near the snack shack, Matt bent toward her ear. "You smell wonderful," he murmured.

She would have raised her face to his for a quick kiss, but a high-pitched voice intruded on the moment.

"You-hoo," that voice sang behind them.

Taylor looked around.

The woman, the Little League's treasurer, scurried toward them. A round, dark-haired woman with a propensity for loud clothes and large costume jewelry, she pointed a bejeweled finger at Taylor. "I'm afraid we can't find your paper from the doctor. We don't have a record of one for your son."

Her son. "He's not my son," she said, but she could have told the woman that he held no less place in her heart than her own child would. "I'm his aunt."

"Oh." In a speculative manner, she cocked a brow. "I thought you two were his parents. Mrs. Grumbee pointed you out when I asked someone where to find you."

From her purse, Taylor withdrew the original of the doctor's okay and presented it to the woman. She didn't dare look Matt's way. If he looked troubled by the woman's mistake about them, her good mood would dip. Better she didn't look, didn't know his reaction. She wanted everything he didn't. Promises. Marriage. Permanency. And unless he changed his mind, she sensed they'd have nothing.

"This is fine. Thank you," the woman was saying, cutting into her thoughts.

When the woman turned away, Taylor resumed climbing the bleachers. Though edgy about what Matt might be thinking, she refused to let anything deflate her spirits today. This day was too important to Petey. "Is this all right?" she asked about the bleacher she'd chosen.

"It's fine," Matt assured her. He cast a glance around, wondering how many other people assumed as the woman had that they were Petey's parents. The idea should have bothered him. Why didn't it? he wondered.

With pride and enjoyment, Taylor watched Petey race to his position when the team he was on took the field. All business, he stood in right field, his mitt ready for action. "Look," she urged Matt, and pointed toward left field.

Tracing her stare, Matt chuckled. The boy in left field was batting his hat at bugs. The center fielder was sitting down while the third baseman was waving at his mom.

On the bleacher in front of them, the second baseman's father called out instructions. "Steven, don't forget." He pointed toward first base. "Throw the ball that way."

His son didn't listen. But then, none of the other players did, either, minutes later when the first batter swung. He hit the rubber portion of the T below the ball. Though the ball fell only inches from the T, the batter took off, running toward third base.

"Wrong way," the coach shouted.

"Go the other way," someone else yelled.

With the boy's frantic U-turn, cheers began and grew louder until he reached first base. The next batter's swing proved more accurate. It connected with the ball and sent it flying between third base and shortstop.

People in the stands cheered.

On the field, chaos began. The left fielder, the center fielder and Petey in right field all raced toward the ball. As they nearly collided, the second baseman scooped up the ball and threw it to third base. The ball bounced just short of third base, then rolled toward the dugout. In foul territory, the third baseman was in pursuit of the shortstop who had his hat.

Throughout the game, spectators clapped and yelled. The game never had a dull moment. The second baseman kept sitting down, and the third baseman got distracted by a low-flying airplane. More batters hit balls. Though catches were missed, sailing over heads and between legs, encouraging cheers rang out for the team's effort.

Taylor couldn't recall laughing so much. "I'm still stunned that they won," she whispered to Matt when they wandered along with team members and their families to the school's gymnasium after the game for a special get-together.

"Don't let Petey hear you," Matt said low, inching with her along the buffet table.

Behind her, Petey was chatting with a teammate named Jimmy.

Her plate filled with pasta and pizza, Taylor scanned the large room for seats at one of the long tables. She took only a couple of steps into the aisle.

Coming toward her, two boys carrying their plates of spaghetti jockeyed for the lead.

"Let me go first," the one boy said, crowding the other.

"No, I'm first," the other insisted.

A push, another shove, and elbows collided. Spaghetti sailed from the one boy's plate. Taylor jumped back, but not quickly enough. Red noodles hit the front of her skirt. Some plopped on the floor, some slithered down, a few stuck to her skirt.

"Oh, gosh!" The boy with the empty plate looked terrified.

The boy's buddy gloated. "Man, are you in trouble."

Shocked, she stared down at the mess for only a second.

"What can I do?" Matt asked, beside her now. He looked torn between concern and laughter.

She never answered. Laughter bubbled out of her. If only her friends could see her now, she mused, holding her arms out. In her life, she'd had a lot of unique experiences. This, she thought, was one she doubted she would ever forget.

Matt felt himself slipping over an edge at that moment. Most women would have been upset, if not infuriated. But she was laughing hard at herself.

Holding his empty plate, the boy stood frozen before her. "I'm real sorry," he said over Taylor's sniffs as she worked at composing herself.

She met his wide eyes, feeling sorry for him. She recalled an accident when she was six. She'd hurried behind her mother to catch her and get a goodbye kiss before she'd left for the opera. Getting too close, Taylor had tripped. She'd reached out for anything to stop her fall. Unfortunately she'd grabbed her mother's designer original. The velvet had ripped. Her mother had been furious, sending her to her room in tears. "It's all right," she said now to the boy. "Once I dropped a cupcake on a lady's head."

A faint, hesitant smile curved the corners of his lips. "Really?"

"Really," she assured him.

He gave her another weak smile, looking relieved she'd made the same mistake.

Nothing could be gained from dragging out the situation, Taylor decided. "You'd better get some more food," she urged, sending him on his way.

One of the dinner's organizers, bringing a mop, tapped Matt's shoulder. "That's some lady," he said in a low voice.

Matt didn't need anyone to tell him that. "Was that a true story?" he asked Taylor as they skirted the mess on the floor.

Taylor gave a sigh at the red stain on her skirt. "I really didn't know what else to say to make the boy feel better."

What she hadn't said came through clearly. The boy's feelings had mattered most.

"Have I told you yet that you're pretty special?"

Taylor sent him a quick smile. "I never get tired of hearing it."

Just to make some kind of contact, he curled his hand over hers. "I'll tell you again later then."

"After I do something about this," she said with another, softer laugh, intending to go to the rest room. "I must look a mess."

Remembering the relief on the kid's face, Matt didn't think she'd ever looked lovelier. "Spaghetti sauce is becoming."

"Silver-tongued, aren't you?" she teased, humor dancing in her eyes.

What he might be is hooked, Matt realized.

That thought returned at the end of the evening's dinner. Strolling beside him in the parking lot, she was all smiles, looking as if she'd had the best time of her life.

"There it is," Petey said, and pointed at the truck. He turned to Matt. "Guess what?"

Knowing what he planned to tell Matt, Taylor smiled over the proud expression on his face.

"Aunt Taylor is going to be our team mother," he said excitedly, sounding as if she'd been elected President of the United States.

The whole situation still amused her.

In step with Matt, she released one of those smoky laughs that made him think of quieter, more intimate moments with her.

"I've chaired fund-raisers." She shrugged then. "I should be able to run a candy drive."

Matt brushed her hip with his to steer her to the

other side of the parked cars. "Is that one of the jobs you volunteered for?"

Taylor slanted a look up at him. "I didn't exactly volunteer."

Petey piped in, "The kids on the team na-miously—"

"Unanimously," Taylor corrected, sidestepping a puddle left over from the last rain.

"Yeah, that," he said.

"They chose me while I was in the bathroom." Like a bullfighter displaying his cape, Taylor held out her red-stained skirt. "They decided I'd be fun."

Petey proudly beamed at her. "Because she's a good sport."

Matt waited for Petey to climb in the truck, then leaned close and kissed Taylor's nose. "Makes perfect sense to me."

When they stepped into the house, a shocked Lottie wanted to know what happened to Taylor's skirt.

"It looks starched, doesn't it?" Taylor asked, studying it in the foyer mirror. Where the spaghetti sauce had dried on her skirt, the material had stiffened. "I need to get out of this."

In a caress filled more with tenderness than seduction, Matt set his hand at her waist. "I'd be willing to help," he whispered.

"Shh." She glanced at Petey and Lottie.

The older woman, her expression filled with delight, appeared entranced with Petey's account of the ball he hit way out into the outfield. She beamed. "You did wonderful, Master Petey."

"That's because you practiced so much," Taylor reminded him.

"Uh-huh," he said, bobbing his head. Though he didn't always tell time with accuracy, he knew where the hands on the clock pointed when it was his bedtime. "I don't have to go to bed yet, do I?"

Taylor thought he needed some unwinding time. "No, not yet." She slanted a look at Matt. "You'll stay?"

He grinned, the gleam in his eyes assuring her he had something in mind. "I'll stay."

Returning a smile, she wiggled fingers at him in a wave. "I'm going to change."

As she left them, Matt thought about how easily he'd said that. What they'd had was supposed to be only a temporary relationship. That was safe. But he was with them almost daily now. And suddenly he was thinking about something more permanent.

"Matt?" Petey had peeled off the shirt of his uniform. Barefoot, too, he grabbed his hand. "I got a new book. It's bad. Can you read it to me? I can't read it myself yet, but I really, really like it."

Matt chuckled as he found himself being tugged toward the sofa. "What's it about?" he asked, dropping to the sofa with him.

"Animals." Petey bounced on the cushion beside him, then settled in close against his side. "I like it because it had flaps, and there's things behind the flaps."

"Good reason." Matt opened the book about a train carrying animals that played hide-and-seek.

"See this?" Lowering his head, Petey pointed to a page with a shed. "Know what's behind the doors?"

"What?"

"Well, you got to guess. That's what Aunt Taylor said. She said that's part of the fun."

Matt played along. "Okay. Maybe there's an elephant."

Petey looked aghast. "Matt, it can't be an elephant. It says who…"

Amusement rippled through him at the boy's admonishing tone. "If you can't read, how do you know that?"

"I know." Petey delivered a confident grin. "Anyway, elephants don't say whooo."

"What does?"

"Owls." He opened the flap to reveal one.

Matt got the impression he'd memorized the book. "Guess you know then what's on this page," he said, turning it. "Something is shaking the bush," Matt read. "Grrr, it says."

"It's a bear," Petey said with authority.

"Tell me what's in the freight car going squawk, squawk then?"

"That's easy. It's a bird."

Matt draped an arm around Petey's shoulder, and with his other hand, he lifted the flap to reveal colorful birds. "Parrots."

Petey cuddled closer. "I knew that."

Taylor stood in the doorway listening. Petey snuggled in the crook of Matt's arm as if he belonged there. How could Matt not see what was so obvious? They belonged together. "It's time for bed."

As Petey moaned a protest, to sidetrack him from making a fuss, Matt tapped one of his own shoulders. "Come on. Hop on. I'll carry you in." Lifting him to his shoulders first, Matt sprinted down the hallway and into the bedroom, then with Petey laughing, he dumped him on the bed.

While Petey wiggled into his Superman pajamas, Matt stepped back from the bed to let Taylor take over. From the doorway he watched them go through a ritual that included teeth brushing and prayers. Sure he could have left, but the truth was he wanted to be a part of this moment.

In what Taylor viewed as a stall tactic, Petey said good-night to each of the action figures on the dresser. After he settled on the bed, she thought he would crawl under the covers. Instead he spotted Matt and darted across the room to him. "'Night, Matt."

Matt dropped to his haunches for Petey's hug. "'Night, champ."

The thin arms tightened around his neck. "I love you."

Matt didn't say anything—couldn't. Three little words nearly rocked him back on his heels. He hadn't counted on this. Hell, say it like it is. He'd never expected he would fall for the kid, too. He held him longer than he planned and not as long as he would have liked. "Good night, Petey." As Petey shot back to the bed, Matt turned on his heel and left the room.

Taylor guessed Petey had given him plenty to think about. She tucked Petey under the comforter, then kissed him. No ties, Matt had told her. But something invisible already bound the three of them.

She left the bedroom to find Matt standing near the terrace doors in the dimly lit living room. She noted that he'd turned on only one lamp. His back to her, he was staring out at the dark yard.

On other nights they'd sat late at night with the lights out and watched an old movie. Since he planned to stay, she flicked on the television. "I don't know what's on."

Matt couldn't talk, not yet. With the hug, the boy's kiss on his cheek and those words, something had twisted in the vicinity of his heart. He'd left the room, trying to settle scrambled emotions. This wasn't just about now. As if it were yesterday, one memory from five years ago descended on him. With it came the anger, the ache, the emptiness.

Too quiet, Taylor mused. Puzzled, she moved closer, noticed then that he was staring at the photo of Jared and Elizabeth and Petey. "That's the last one I have of them."

"A nice-looking family."

"He'll look like Jared when he grows up," she said. She'd noted before the resemblance. Petey even had some of Jared's mannerisms, like the way he tipped his head in a questioning way when uncertain about something.

"Do you think most boys resemble their fathers?"

Taylor considered the question for a second. "I don't know. Why?"

"I had a son."

Just like that he'd said it. Only a few feet from him, she stopped dead in her tracks, wondering if she'd misunderstood. "What did you say?"

Matt raised his eyes to meet her stare. "I had a son." Saying the words aloud weren't any easier now than they'd been five years ago.

Without looking away from him, Taylor switched off the television.

"I didn't know." He stood stoically before her. "Alisha hadn't told me."

Taylor barely breathed at the depth of sadness clouding his eyes.

"When my business failed, she split."

Taylor didn't want to know about the business. He'd said a child. She wanted to know about the child.

"After—a month later, she called me. That's when I learned she'd been pregnant." He looked away, past her at nothing. "She told me then that she'd had an abortion."

He had truly hated her that night, Matt remembered. She'd called and had simply stated the facts. She'd been pregnant; she wasn't now. And by the way, it was a boy. He'd wanted to scream at the world. He'd walked in the rain for hours that night. He'd gotten drunk. He'd wallowed in the pain of his loss. Nothing had helped. He'd had a son.

Now he drew a hard breath to will away the rush of emotion revisiting him. Never would he see him, hear his voice, laugh with him.

Taylor took the breath she hadn't known she'd been holding as she agonized for him. He'd been hurt so badly. No wonder his sister had disliked her when they'd first met. She'd been afraid for her brother. She'd wanted to protect Matt. Cara had known what was now clear to Taylor, what she'd seen in his eyes only minutes ago. He'd had his heart torn open.

Afraid he'd close her out now, she put herself in front of him and touched his cheek to force his eyes to meet hers. Just as she shared his joy, she felt his pain. "Matt, I'm sorry."

She was gentle, so damn gentle.

He might not expect this to be for more than this moment, but Taylor slipped her arms around him, knowing that no other man would ever have so much of her heart.

As her touch soothed, the sweet scent of her filled him. He would never forget that part of his past, Matt knew. But this woman was easing away the bitterness. He felt peace. Here, in her arms, with her mouth on his.

"Let me love you," she murmured against his lips.

A sweet pang of longing pulled at him; he said nothing. He simply lifted her into his arms and carried her into the darkness of her bedroom. Kneeling with her on the bed, he drew off the scoop-necked T-shirt. He wanted to say words to her, tell her she was helping to blur the memory, tell her she was all he longed for, but when her lips met his, thoughts tumbled from his mind.

As they sank back on the bed, Taylor wedged a hand between them and pulled at his shirt. More than passion burned within her. She loved him. She had no doubt. An avalanche of emotion swept over her when he was near.

Breaths blending, they tugged at jeans, yanking denim down. Then with a slowness meant to drive her mad, his fingers lowered her panties, and all the while his mouth trailed a path to her belly. Whispering her name, he stirred her with a stroke of his hand, or a brush of his mouth. There wasn't a world outside. Problems didn't exist. They belonged together.

Again his lips fastened on hers. No talking was needed. Growing greedy, she gripped the muscular flesh of his hip, the hardness of his thigh.

The seduction she'd begun, he continued. His lips caressed her breasts, circled each nipple before moving lower. Taylor strained against his hand, which sought now the moistness between her thighs, then pleasured her, luring her down a path of excitement.

Lost in a cloud of sensation, she sighed his name. Passion blended with the love consuming her. Shifting, she pressed her mouth to his chest, let her tongue moisten his skin, then she took control.

Wild for the heat and fullness of him, she straddled him and slowly drew him into her. This went beyond desire. They were more than lovers. Regardless of what he believed, she felt his love in every gentle kiss, every tender caress. In his arms, with him like this, she believed in their love, was certain it would last.

Hot, her head swimming, she strained toward him, arching her back. Weakness and strength melding, she murmured his name as the frenzy began. She wished she could tell him what he meant to her, say the words of love she felt, but she was breathless, trembling with the passion that bound them.

Speaking was impossible. Sensations slithered

through her. For a few earth-shattering seconds, she blended with him, creating a oneness that she knew could never happen with any other man. As her world spun, she realized she would always be his.

Chapter Twelve

Sunlight pierced the bedroom through the filmy white curtains. Matt lay in a jumble of pale pink sheets and didn't move. As Taylor curled even closer, draping a leg over his, he savored the warmth and feminine softness against him. He also faced his own dilemma. He'd been so certain that he could keep emotion at bay. But she'd come into his life with her smiles, her laughter, her tenderness, and all his good intentions about no involvement had dissolved.

"We should get up," she said sleepily, breaking into his thoughts.

Lightly he toyed with the tips of her tousled hair while he angled his head to see her. Her face pale in the morning light, her mouth slightly parted, she looked enticing. Even in sleep, she made a yearning flare within him that he'd nearly forgotten. He would have liked to stay in bed with her, do nothing but stare at her. Languidly he ran his fingers down her thigh. "Why?"

"Petey," she said simply, sleepily.

He needed no further explanation. He recalled one morning last week when he'd barely snuck out of her bedroom in time before Petey ran in. It occurred to him that he'd never had this kind of conversation with any other woman. None of them had had children. There had never been anyone else to consider. Effortlessly he could imagine waking every morning with her, seeing the boy at breakfast, listening to his chatter. It would be easy to believe in this woman, he knew, and in love again.

"Matt, we really need to—"

"Get up," he finished for her. Though thoughts of lazing around were still on his mind, he eased himself away from her. "Go back to sleep."

"No, I should get up," she said, but as she spoke, she nestled deeper beneath the sheet.

Tenderness filling him, Matt stared down at her and smiled. "I can see how hard you're trying." Before he changed his mind and crawled back under the sheet, he padded to the shower.

Minutes later, showered and dressed, he stopped by the bed and bent over to kiss her. "I'll check on Petey," he said softly.

What he interpreted as a pleasurable sigh slipped from her lips. "Hmmm. Okay."

Smiling, Matt left the room. The boy, too, mattered to him more than he'd expected. At first, he'd been drawn to the child, a five-year-old like the one he could have had. But Petey was too unique to be a substitute for anyone. He'd charmed Matt. He'd made him care.

Entering the bedroom, Matt found him, dressed in only jeans, kneeling on the bed and thumbing through a comic book.

With a look up, he tossed Matt a broad grin. "Are we really going to spend the day at your place, Matt?" he asked while scrambling off the bed.

Matt scanned the bedroom. It looked different in daylight. He noted socks were strewn over the floor, several shirts spilled over the top of a dresser drawer, and a towel draped the rim of the hamper. A glance at the bathroom revealed that he wasn't the only one who squeezed the toothpaste tube in the middle. "Your aunt told you we were going out tonight, didn't she?"

Petey dropped to his knees beside the bed and wiggled on his belly halfway under it. "Uh-huh." Muffled words continued. "She said your sister was going to baby-sit because Lottie can't and Leeland is visiting his brother. I met your sister at the birthday party."

"That's right. Her name is Cara."

"Is she nice?" he asked, popping out from under the bed with a sneaker in his hand.

Matt spotted the other one across the room. "She likes kids," he offered as a reassurance. That was the truth. And Cara had been agreeable to taking the job when Matt had phoned her yesterday morning.

By his dresser now, he yanked open a drawer. "What should I wear today?"

"Anything," Matt answered. He'd be stuck in a monkey suit tonight. Knowing they'd be away, he and Taylor had decided to devote the day to Petey.

Petey pulled on a shirt he'd retrieved from the drawer. Sitting on the floor now, head bent, he concentrated on his shoelaces. "Where are you going tonight?"

Matt gathered a few socks from the floor and tossed them in the hamper. "Your aunt wants to go to a party."

The boy's brows veed while he struggled with the shoelace. "With cake and balloons and games?"

"I doubt that. It's a party to raise money, a fundraiser." Matt eyed the stack of comic books on a shelf of the corner bookcase. He'd passed some of the best time of his youth soaking up the adventures of Superman or the antics of Mickey Mouse. He hadn't been particular. He'd loved reading them. As an adult, he could contently spend hours reading a book.

"Will you get ice cream?"

"I don't think so."

Petey wrinkled his nose. "I'm glad I don't have to go." He tugged at his top lip as he tried again to tie his right sneaker. "It doesn't sound like fun."

Matt had his doubts, too.

Taylor only remained in bed until the door closed behind Matt. Though she'd been tempted to curl into the mattress, in a semi-awake state, she'd known it was only a matter of minutes before Petey rushed in to get her up.

Wearing shorts and a pale blue, midriff-length

blouse, she wandered toward the kitchen. She felt wonderful, in love. And wondering where they went from here. Mostly she wondered how to convince Matt that they all belonged together.

Setting a palm against the kitchen's swinging door, she breezed in and instantly felt a warmth rush her. This was family. At the table, Matt sat with a blueberry muffin in front of him, the newspaper folded to the crossword puzzle. Grinning at her, Petey was hunched over a cereal bowl of multicolored, dimesize balls swimming in milk. Over her shoulder at the oven, Lottie beamed while she removed a pan of muffins from the oven. And Leeland, looking more relaxed than she'd ever seen him, was perched on a nearby stool, appearing to have nothing to do but enjoy the conversation.

"Matt's eating all the muffins," Petey announced between mouthfuls of cereal.

Matt sent him an amused look. He hadn't wasted any time to play snitch, now that he had someone to tell. "I saved you *one*." Matt had sensed her nearness before she'd come in. Minus makeup, she looked pale, fragile. She stood in the soft glow of morning sunlight. Without doing anything, she enticed him, made him yearn to hold her. It was as if a part of him, missing, had suddenly returned.

"I made plenty," Lottie assured them. "I'll get some more."

Petey sent her another sunny smile. "Matt said that we're going to eat lunch at his house."

So they'd already made plans, she thought, pleased. Last week, after a day at a nearby amusement park, they'd gone to Matt's apartment. It didn't matter to her where they were as long as they were together.

"Want some cereal?" Petey asked, making her aware that she'd been lost in thought, staring down at his bowl.

Pink, purple and green cereal didn't appeal to her. "No, thank you." Walking past him, she touched the top of his head. "But I'll have coffee," she said with a glance at Leeland before she stepped up close behind Matt. Bending forward, she slipped her arms around his neck. Deliberately she let his lips tickle his ear. "How much of the crossword puzzle did you get done?" She'd learned he was a fanatic about completing it.

Matt angled his face toward her and stole a quick kiss. "It's done." God, he wanted to believe in them, he realized. When he'd started with her, he'd expected an end, but at some moment, she'd forced him to rethink his plan. Why couldn't this work? was the big question now. What was decided on before wasn't etched in stone.

Taylor pecked his cheek. Without him saying a word to her, with just a simple look, she felt caressed by him. Even when they were with other people, he could make her feel as if they were alone.

"I had help," Matt said about the crossword puzzle, and cast a grin at Lottie. "Without her, I couldn't have finished. She knew who the silent-screen star named Betty was. Betty Boop."

"Oh, go on," she said about his tease.

Nearby, Leeland politely chuckled.

"Matt said we're having hamburgers for lunch."

Petey made much about the crunchy texture of the cereal in his bowl, taking one piece at a time into his mouth and crunching slowly and exaggerated on it.

"Are you cooking?" Taylor asked as she took a seat across the table from Matt.

Matt cracked a grin. He decided that she looked awfully cute with her hair tucked up, held by a comb, several errant strands framing her face. "There isn't anyone else to do it, is there?"

Taylor looked up with a thank-you smile for Leeland as he set a cup of coffee before her. "My cooking talents aren't so bad. I made lasagna." Not too discreetly, she winked at Lottie. They all knew who'd really done the cooking. "And what about the cake?"

Matt tapped his fingertips at his chest. "Loved it. Best cake I ever had."

A giggle at the ridiculousness of his comment slipped out. "You lie wonderfully."

Petey offered his opinion. "It wasn't too terrible."

"There." She waited until Matt had taken a hearty bite of the muffin and his mouth was full. "Cook extraordinaire."

Petey frowned. "What's that?"

"What I'll never be," Taylor said good-naturedly, then gave him the definition.

Amazingly, while Petey was slurping the last of the milk in his bowl, he was thinking about his next meal. "Can I get a soda for lunch at the grocery store?"

Taylor shot a look at Matt. She hadn't known they were going shopping. "A grocery store?"

"It'll be fun," Petey piped in.

She gave Matt an I'll-wait-and-see look that stirred his laugh. "I guess we're ready. Are you?"

"Always," he quipped, drawing an airy laugh from her. His life used to be a lot simpler. It had also been emptier, he realized.

Fifteen minutes after leaving the house, they were strolling along aisles in a brightly lit, large grocery store. Taylor marveled at what Matt dropped in his cart. "You have the preferences of a ten-year-old," she said when Petey left to pick up a box of cereal.

Matt leveled a pseudo-affronted look at her. "Nothing wrong with any of this." He dropped two packages of chocolate sandwich cookies in the cart that already contained potato chips, marshmallow cupcakes and three packages of brownies. Hearing her groan when he grabbed a bag of spice drops, he laughed. Never before could he recall a time when he'd enjoyed himself so much doing something so ordinary.

In disbelief, Taylor watched him add a box of cherry popsicles to the cart. "You'll pay later in life for doing this to your stomach."

Petey dashed back with the cereal. "Can we get ice cream?"

"Bars?" Matt asked.

Petey's eyes brightened. "Yeah."

With a sigh Taylor gave up any notion of curbing their propensity toward junk food. In the next aisle she paused before the shelves of condiments. A moment passed before she realized he and Petey had moved out of the aisle. Catching up with them in the produce department, she noted with approval that the upper portion of the cart did contain plastic bags of fruits and vegetables.

"I really like watermelon," Petey told him.

"One watermelon coming up." Matt set half a one in the cart. "We'll have a seed-spitting contest," he whispered teasingly in Taylor's ear.

She slanted a you're-kidding look at him. "I don't think so."

"Ah, Taylor, you haven't lived until you've done it."

"I believe I can go my whole life without the experience. Thank you very much."

He loved that regal tone. Hell, he loved everything about her. There it was, wasn't it, he mused, casting a sidelong glance at her. No denial would make him believe otherwise. He loved her. It had to be true. He was admitting it to himself in the middle of a brightly lit grocery store at eleven o'clock in the morning.

When they returned to his apartment, Matt unpacked groceries while Taylor joined Petey in doing a jigsaw puzzle of *The Lion King* that he'd started the last time he'd been at Matt's.

"I'm hungry, Matt," Petey called out.

Taylor wrapped her arm around his shoulder. "When aren't you?" A smile in her eyes, she ambled to Matt.

Standing at the opened refrigerator door, he grinned over the top of it at her while talking to Petey. "Do you want a cheeseburger?"

The boy's fair brows knitted. "If that's what you're having."

Taylor thought his response predictable. He always wanted whatever Matt had. As she came around to peek over Matt's shoulder, he handed back an onion. "Here. You chop while I cook the hamburgers."

"Aye, aye, sir," she said with a salute.

At the table Petey looked up from the puzzle with a giggle.

For both of them it was getting harder not to want to be with Matt all the time, Taylor realized as contentment curled around her like a cocoon.

"Daydreaming isn't going to get you out of the job," Matt teased, setting a knife and a cutting board on the counter for her.

She caught the smile tugging at the corners of his lips, and moved to the counter to get down to business. Chopping anything was a new experience. But she'd ridden a camel in Saudi Arabia and sunbathed at the Riviera and cruised in a hot-air balloon over France. Not everyone had such experiences. Pleasant ones. Far more pleasant than this one, she decided between sniffs. "You could have done this job," she grumbled as tears smarted her eyes.

At the stove, Matt flipped the hamburgers and grinned in her direction. Sharing a simple meal, just having her in his kitchen, was as special a memory as the ones she'd given him in bed.

Taylor had seen that grin. "You're enjoying this, aren't you?"

Matt released a soft, satisfied laugh before he set

down the spatula. He slipped his arms around her from behind. "This is what I'm enjoying."

The smell of onions filled the kitchen while hamburgers sizzled in the pan. Turning in his arms, Taylor pressed her cheek to his and saw Petey smiling. Everything seemed so right at this moment. She wanted this to last. She wanted that more than anything she'd ever longed for.

"Wait until you see the video we got," Petey mumbled between bites of his hamburger when they were sitting at the table later. "We got *Godzilla.*"

Taylor sipped her coffee and listened to them debate who would win if a T-rex and Godzilla fought.

"You agree then. Godzilla wins," Matt said deadly serious, as if the world's future depended on Petey's answer.

"Right. Godzilla wins."

Taylor peered at them over the rim of her cup. Matt winked at her before unstraddling the chair and leaving the table. He would have made a wonderful father, she reflected. No, he *would be* one if he would let himself accept all they'd found.

The sun had set by the time Matt drove them home, then left to dress for the night's charity affair.

While Petey played a computer game, Taylor relaxed in the bath. For too long. Running late, she rushed to the closet. Her mind was filled with possibilities about this evening with Matt. If he felt comfortable, if he had a good time tonight, he might begin to accept that they were meant for each other.

At the trill of the phone, she quickly zipped up her

dress before answering it. Apprehension fluttered inside her that it might be Matt, backing off. Instead her aunt answered her greeting. To keep the conversation brief, Taylor mentioned the fund-raiser.

"Since you're going out, I won't keep you." She sounded like the proverbial cat that had swallowed the canary.

Back at the closet, Taylor hunted for her shoes. She heard the rustle of papers as if her aunt was on a search.

"The reason I called was to tell you that I had him checked."

Taylor shoved around a few shoe boxes. "Who?"

"Your Mr. Duran."

Taylor quickly slid up the sling strap of her shoe, then straightened. "What!"

"Oh, don't be upset with me," she soothed, even though Taylor hadn't said more than one word. "It was necessary."

"No, it wasn't. I don't need him checked on, because I believe in him," she said, determined to make her point.

"With no reservations?" her aunt challenged.

Taylor would admit that she'd had some for a while. She was born with a silver spoon in her mouth and knew that plenty of people wanted to snatch it from her.

As if her answer wasn't needed, her aunt went on. "Well, it doesn't matter now. You may rest easier. For a man of limited means, he's proven to be quite acceptable. Not that I wouldn't have chosen someone else for you, if you'd asked for my advice. But of course, you didn't.''

Taylor relaxed, aware this call was meant to convey her aunt's reluctant acceptance. "If I've never thanked you—''

"Thanked me for what?''

"For being you,'' Taylor said softly.

"Oh.'' The word came out in a strained emotional voice. "Enough of that,'' her aunt said in her gruffer tone. "Now, as I was saying. You knew that he'd been quite successful in construction for several years?''

"Yes, I knew that.''

"And lost his business?''

"Yes, I knew that, too.''

"Because of the partner. This—'' She paused. "Now where is that name? Oh, yes. Harry Kerchel. He simply had no business sense, and lost everything when your Matthew Duran was out of town. Anyway, the important issue isn't how he lost his money. What's important is that my investigators learned what he's been doing since. Several sources have assured me that he wouldn't accept money from you even if you offered. Why, he didn't even file bankruptcy. All this time he's been working to pay off his debts.''

Nothing her aunt said surprised Taylor. From the beginning Taylor had witnessed an honesty in the way Matt was with her and Petey.

"So after the partner lost everything, he made payments to everyone. According to Dempsey,'' she said about her attorney, "he's made the last payment a month ago. A man of that caliber would hardly be after your money. He's—well, I suppose the only words for him are that he's an honorable man.''

"Something Ian St. John is not," she told her aunt.

Only a second of silence passed. "Has something happened with Ian?"

Taylor opened her jewelry box while she summarized her last conversation with Ian when he'd revealed his financial woes.

"Oh, my, his father must be rolling over in his grave," her aunt said solemnly. "What a disgrace to the name of St. John." Her aunt clucked her tongue. "No St. John has ever been a gigolo."

Amused at her aunt's description, Taylor caught herself smiling in the mirror at herself while she fastened her earrings.

"Actually I'm not surprised. I never liked the man."

"You never liked him? I thought you did."

"Your father liked him," she said about her brother. "I thought he had shifty eyes."

Taylor couldn't hold back a laugh. At that moment she felt closer to her aunt than ever before.

"It would appear I'm a good judge of character."

"I always believed that. I remember how much you liked Elizabeth."

"Yes, I did," her aunt admitted quietly.

Taylor let her eyes stray to the photo of Jared, Elizabeth and Petey. She would always remember them like that, laughing. Hearing the door chimes, she said a quick goodbye to her aunt. She checked her reflection before heading to the door, but again she found herself looking at the photograph.

The last time they'd all been together had been at Christmas. After her father had died, she'd welcomed her brother and his family back into the family home.

Taylor left the room and started down the hallway. This past Christmas had been the happiest she'd known. No one had cared that popcorn had gotten spilled or that wrapping paper had been everywhere. They'd had fun. They'd been a family. Her brother had given up nothing all those years ago. He'd had so much more with Elizabeth and Petey than he'd had in his life before them.

He'd found the elusive happiness before he died. He'd found what she wanted.

Half an hour later she and Matt entered the lobby of the hotel in central Phoenix. "I'm glad I didn't have to go alone to this," Taylor whispered to him, wanting him to know she appreciated his going even though he hadn't wanted to.

He'd have done anything for her, Matt mused, his gaze sweeping down the dress that bared one shoulder and dipped low in the back. She left him breathless. It wasn't the first time he'd had a similar reaction to her. Even dressed in jeans and sneakers and a T-shirt, she caused a longing to curl through him. It was an inner beauty, the glow in her face, the sparkle in her eyes, the slow, amused curve of her lips that always made him want to draw her close and kiss her. Right now he wished they were somewhere alone, cheek to cheek, dancing. Bending his head toward hers, he kissed her ear above the teardrop-shaped diamond dangling from it. "I didn't tell you earlier. You look beautiful."

Taylor gave him an appreciative look. "You do, too."

The hand Matt moved to her waist tightened with his laugh. "Right."

"For a man, you look beautiful." She smiled with him, enjoying the private moments even as Matt urged her forward into a room that gleamed beneath crystal chandeliers.

Matt had been to similar gatherings. People of money milled around, women dressed in satin and silk and sequined gowns, men in tuxedos. He knew what to do, how to blend. But he would rather be somewhere else and not in a tuxedo with a too-tight collar.

"Stay close," Taylor appealed lightly as she spotted a woman prone to nonstop chatter weaving her way to them.

Matt planned to. The biggest problem in his life was that he suddenly didn't want to let her go. "So what's the object of this little gathering?"

Taylor lifted a flute of champagne from the tray of a white-jacketed servant passing by. "It's to raise money for the city's art museums by having an auction. This is the most prestigious formal soiree of the social calendar, according to Sarah," she said lightly as the bids began.

"Taylor!" Arms outstretched, the woman who'd been intent on reaching Taylor gushed her name. Closing in, she offered Taylor the obligatory social greeting and grazed her cheek across hers. "It's been so long since we've seen you."

Except for that brief second, the woman's eyes never left Matt. Aware that he was the real reason for her almost neck-breaking jaunt across the room to them, Taylor made the expected introduction.

"I've tried to place you," she said, and pointed a long-nailed finger at Matt. "Are you one of the Boston Durans?"

"My family's from Ohio," he answered to end her speculation he had any blue-blooded connections.

The woman's questioning eyes shifted to Taylor, who said nothing in response, instead steering her into a discussion about a fourteen-karat gold necklace up for bid.

Matt scanned the crowd. He saw Ian St. John across the room, but the man kept his distance. Zeroing in on Taylor and the woman again, he nodded in response to the woman's polite comment about being delighted to meet him. "Tomorrow you'll be the favorite topic for the gossipmongers," he said to Taylor once they were alone.

Taylor dismissed his remark with a shrug and leaned closer. She'd felt stares when they'd first arrived. She could care less if the morning gossip was about them, about her. "I don't care what they say."

She was saying that now. Alisha had said almost the same words when they started seeing each other, Matt remembered.

Taylor traced the deepening crease between his brows. "You're frowning."

"I'm hungry," he said as an excuse. If he mentioned the doubts that had come to mind even fleetingly, he'd have snatched away her smile.

"Can't have that," she said lightly about his previous comment. "You snarl when you're hungry."

Though Matt could think of a dozen other places

he'd like to be with her, after a walk down the buffet line, he had to admit that at least the food was good.

"Want a taste of this?" Taylor asked, intruding on his thoughts and offering him a forkful of crab salad.

He shook his head. "What is that green stuff on your plate?"

"I have no idea."

Matt pulled a face. "Adventurous, aren't you?"

In an impish mood, she sidled closer. "I'll show you later," she said distractedly, looking away in response to someone calling her name. Across the room, Sarah beckoned to her. "I'll be right back."

"I'll hold you to that," Matt said, but he doubted she'd be back quickly. After the auction they'd spent time with Sarah and her main squeeze, some guy named Brett. Matt liked both of them, especially the talkative, airy Sarah. Talkative was the best word to describe her. Watching Taylor glide toward her friend now, he expected the conversation to take a while.

Growing anxious to leave, he eased his way past couples to the double doors. Around him, people chattered about the America's Cup, about a lawyer with political aspirations, about a woman hostessing a small informal party for a pianist. So much of the evening mirrored ones he'd endured with Alisha.

Anxious to leave now, he turned back to wait for Taylor and nearly plowed into another woman. Fate wasn't kind, he decided as he stared at a face from his past.

Chapter Thirteen

The woman before him carried the same cold expression he remembered five years ago. Ursula Marscroft hadn't changed. Her gray hair pinned severely back, she wore a diamond necklace that Matt would guess cost more than he'd made last year. Alisha's mother had never liked him. "What are you doing here?" she asked.

No hello. No polite pleasantries. Matt shouldn't have been surprised. "I'm here with someone." He noticed the tasteful name card pinned to her dress near her shoulder, indicating she'd been a planner for the event.

Her eyes narrowing, she drilled Matt with a look that would have bored a hole through a lesser man. "You don't belong here."

Across the room, listening to Sarah expounding

about some woman's contributions to promote funding for the symphony, Taylor stole a glance toward Matt. The woman who'd been talking to him had left. As his eyes briefly made contact with hers, she noted the stiff straightness of his back.

"So what do you think?" Sarah asked.

"What?" Taylor was torn. She saw Matt weaving his way around clusters of people and heading for the outside glass doors. Quickly she excused herself. She sensed more than his purposeful stride putting distance between them. Feet from the doors, she caught up with him. "Who were you talking to?"

Matt stilled, sent her a puzzled look. "You don't know?" It had annoyed the hell out of him that she'd invited him and never told him Ursula was on the fund-raising committee.

The anger was unexpected. Treading carefully, Taylor laced her fingers with his. "This is Sarah's pet project, not mine, so I don't know everyone who's involved. Who is she?" She saw indecision in his face, doubts. That hurt her. She'd thought they'd come so far. In that instant she knew they'd just back-pedaled to the first day when he'd looked at her with distrust because he'd seen Alisha, not her. "Who is she?" she asked again, wondering who could have such an undeniable and immediate effect on him.

Under his breath Matt muttered an oath. She hadn't deserved the anger that had come with such surprising quickness. "Alisha's mother." Full circle, he realized. He'd come full circle. Alisha's mother had said little, but she'd forced him to see more clearly. Another woman. Another time. But everything else was too much the same. He may fit in, but he and Taylor weren't right for each other. He'd almost forgotten. He'd been so damn close to saying words of love to her. "Can you leave?" he asked.

A strange tenseness strained his features. "Yes, of course." His hand touched her elbow, but she felt him pushing her away. In silence she walked to the door with him. Taylor produced a smile for several people she passed. He didn't need to say more. She felt the change in him. His jaw tense, he seemed engaged in a private battle.

Outside, Matt spoke to the parking valet. Waiting for the car, he dealt with conflicting emotions. He wanted to draw her against him; he wanted to distance himself from her. Mentally he shook his head as he observed the parking valet approaching them. "The car is here," Matt said, putting pressure at the small of Taylor's back.

Troubled, she followed the command of his hand and moved forward. She gave him space, time alone with his thoughts while they drove to her house. But her mind was busy. What had she missed? Had something happened she wasn't aware of? Or was this simply because of a chance meeting with someone from his past?

Driving, Matt kept his eyes on the dark street, not even trying to converse. After the breakup with Alisha, he'd come to his senses, seen how inevitable the breakup was. The old cliché about oil and water not mixing rang true. In time that would happen again, he knew. Nothing with Taylor was meant to last, could last.

As he pulled into the driveway, even beneath the mantle of night, he could see the garage, rebuilt, completed. The job was almost finished and so was what he'd foolishly started with Taylor. Whatever they'd found wouldn't work for the long haul. He couldn't fantasize anymore. Seeing Alisha's mother reminded him of what hadn't worked the last time. He'd been stupid to think it would be different with Taylor.

"Are you going to talk to me?" she asked softly when he braked on the curving driveway in front of her home. "We could go in the kitchen for a late snack?" On another evening, one filled with laughter and kisses, they'd puttered in the kitchen making grilled cheese sandwiches. "Lottie's probably in bed, but we did okay before." She knew she was rambling, but with nerves coiled tight, she'd searched for a reminder of a more pleasant evening.

"It's not a good idea, Taylor."

Just like that. How cavalier he sounded. She drew a deep breath, attempting to stay calm. "What are you doing?" she asked with some impatience, but the question wasn't necessary. It was clear he was going to hurt her. "What did she say to you?"

He held the keys to her Mercedes out to her. "The truth."

Taylor took the keys. "What truth?"

"Come on, Taylor." He was fighting himself and all he felt for her. "We both knew how different our lives are. She reminded me about what I'd forgotten. I don't belong with you."

She viewed his reason as a lame excuse. All night he'd been at her side, blending in. Unclipping her seat belt, she watched him slide out from behind the steering wheel. By the time he came around the front of the car, she was standing beside it.

Clouds had gathered, covering the moon. The hem of her dress flapped beneath a strong breeze. With his quietness, she nervously brushed back tendrils of hair flying across her face. Too many thoughts, too many feelings bombarded her. She consciously had to draw a breath. She'd begun to believe in them, in the future. Holding the keys tightly, she felt the metal digging into her palm. "It's over. Is that what you're really saying?"

Matt realized there was no easy way. He wanted to be the sensible one. What was the point in going on like this? There was no future. "Neither of us expected more."

Stupid. She'd believed in something no Elmhurst would ever have. Even Jared, who'd found it all, hadn't lived long enough to enjoy the forever kind of love. No, she'd been an idiot to believe anyone in her family could have more than what money could buy. "I did," she said simply. As she fought the weakness rushing at her, pride rose within her quickly. She remembered now the look on his face earlier. The distrust had been back. That hurt, worse than she was prepared for. Suddenly tired, she curled her fingers tighter around the keys. With nothing to lose, she said what was in her heart. "I love you. But that's not enough. You won't forget that I'm not Alisha."

Matt stared into her eyes, which were dark and moist with anger and hurt. "I didn't mean to hurt you, Taylor."

"Perhaps you didn't. But you always expected this to end. I didn't," she said, then turned away. Desperate for a quick escape, she gave him no time to say more. There was no need. He'd said enough.

It felt like the longest week of her life—a week of tossing and turning, of staring at the dark ceiling, of facing more than she wanted to. Each night in the darkness, with the quiet around her, her eyes would fill with the tears she swore she wouldn't shed. No amount of understanding eased the ache in her chest. She knew that Petey was concerned about Matt's absence, but she was thankful he didn't ask too many questions. She honestly didn't know what to tell him. How could she when she was so confused herself?

When she awoke one morning, exactly seven days since she'd last seen Matt, she felt the full intensity of her heartbreak. She and Petey loved him. He did belong with them. But Matt's vision remained clouded by another woman who'd never understood love was a gift.

Hearing the sounds of others—Leeland's footsteps in the hallway, Petey's television tuned to a cartoon—she eased from the bed. Depressed, she fought the lump in her throat, swallowing hard, refusing to cry, and forced herself to dress for Petey's T-ball game. Regardless of what had happened between her and Matt, Petey didn't need to be subjected to any more of her melancholy.

Once dressed, she wandered to his room, expecting him to be dressed in his uniform. She found the room empty, the shirt to his uniform and his cap on the bed. Puzzled, Taylor began her search.

Several minutes later she spotted him in the living room. Looking as if he had nowhere to go, he was curled up in a corner of the sofa and staring at the television. "What are you doing? You need to get dressed to go to your ball game."

"I don't want to go."

Something weighty settled in the pit of her stomach as she slowly stepped closer. "Don't you feel well?"

"I'm okay," he said. But he didn't look okay.

Bending near, Taylor placed her palm on his forehead. It was cool. No longer concerned he was sick, she sat on the cushion beside him. "Petey, what's wrong?"

His blue eyes filled with bewilderment. "Matt's gone, isn't he?"

How final the words sounded. Taylor drew a long breath. "He's done with his job."

"He's not coming back, is he?" His bottom lip quivered slightly. "Just like mommy and daddy."

Taylor's stomach clenched. "Oh, Petey. This isn't the same." He seemed to have handled their deaths so well. She should have realized that he hadn't grieved long enough. "Honey, this is different," she said about Matt's leaving.

His head snapped up. He stubbornly thrust out his chin. "No, it isn't. He left just like them."

"They didn't want to." How could she explain? How could she not have seen that all this time he'd held this within him?

"Why did Matt?" Tears filled his eyes. "He never

comes to see me. He hasn't for a long, long time,'' he said about the days that had passed.

Taylor drew him into her arms and cradled him close. She had never considered this kind of attachment between them when she'd asked Matt to help. How could she have been so stupid?

"Will you leave, too?"

"No. I won't." She pulled back to look at him. "Why would you think that?"

"Cause I love you."

And everyone he loved left him. "Oh, Petey." Her throat tightened. Gathering him in her arms again, she drew a hard breath. "I'm not leaving," she promised.

Get on with your life. That had been Matt's first thought for the past week. This morning he was awake at daybreak. Before seven he'd estimated a new job in Phoenix to build a wooden deck and a gazebo. Before nine he'd delivered more of his carvings to Lannie Esten's gallery. The show was scheduled for a Friday several weeks away. Now all he had to do was pick up his life and pretend Taylor and Petey had never been a part of it.

How could he when he couldn't forget the hurt he'd seen in her eyes? He hadn't wanted to hurt her. He loved her. But her life-style wasn't his. Like it or not, her money made the difference. Because of it, hadn't Alisha thought she could do anything she wanted? Hadn't she split him open with her game playing? And left him hollow with her decision to take away the child he'd have treasured?

In his kitchen he poured coffee in a cup. Taylor

would go on with her life. Eventually she would fall in love and marry someone more acceptable for her.

That thought brought no solace. Matt swore ripely and dumped the coffee in the sink without taking a sip. In passing, he slammed a kitchen cupboard door harder than necessary.

"Maybe I should leave," Cara said behind him in response to the outburst.

He took a hard breath before he greeted her.

"Do you have anything to eat? I'm really hungry." Breezing past him, she pursed her lips as if she'd swallowed something sour. "You look awful."

"Tired." Idly he ran fingers across his unshaven jaw. "I need to shave." He wanted to be alone. But if he insisted on that, she would feel compelled to stay, to try to learn what was wrong, to help cheer him up.

"How come you haven't returned my phone calls? Is something the matter?" She studied him closely.

"I've been busy."

"Busy?"

He looked up to see her holding the refrigerator door open. In her other hand was the last slice of the cake Petey and Taylor had made for him.

"How old is this cake?"

"I should have thrown it out. Taylor made it over a week ago."

His sister did a U-turn. "She really baked a cake for you?"

Matt rubbed at the back of his neck. A nagging headache had begun a few minutes ago. "So?"

"Are you being deliberately dense? She must really love you."

She claimed she did, but so had Alisha, Matt reminded himself.

Standing by the counter, Cara gazed at the stale cake. "I've never baked a cake for any man."

Maybe he *was* being dense today. "What aren't you saying?"

"I bet you were pleased."

At the time he'd been.

"Have you ever had another woman do something like that for you?" She didn't wait for a response. "And she didn't know how, but she did it anyway. Right?"

Matt merely nodded.

"See. That says it all."

He turned away with a shake of his head.

"Wait a minute." Her frown deepening, she abandoned the cake. "What's going on here?"

As he expected, her radar had picked up that all was not blissful in his life. "Nothing."

"Oh, Matt. You stopped seeing her?"

She didn't understand, wouldn't. "Save it," he said, not interested in any advice from anyone. "I thought you didn't like her."

"I wasn't sure about her before, but I am now."

"Why? Because of a cake?" He decided she was losing it.

"Yes, because of the cake. This woman, who probably never spent an hour in the kitchen in her whole life, tackled the job of baking you a cake. Why would she do that if she didn't love you? Alisha wouldn't."

No, Alisha wouldn't. She wouldn't do anything Taylor had. The woman who'd made that cake was the same one who'd grabbed a baseball mitt and gotten dirty playing catch with a little boy, who'd had a spaghetti dinner dumped in her lap and good-naturedly laughed rather than spoil the evening, who'd gotten sticky with frosting just for the sake of a little boy's laughter. That woman had been nothing like the spoiled woman Alisha had been. *I'm not Alisha,* Taylor had said.

"Matt, are you going to answer it?" His sister stood in front of him, her head tipped slightly to the side. "The telephone," she added when he focused on her.

Under his breath, he muttered an expletive for daydreaming, but he couldn't shake away his own thought. Taylor wasn't anything like Alisha. When had he mixed them up? he wondered while he snatched up the telephone receiver. Why had he?

Nothing prepared him for the voice that answered his greeting.

"Matt, it's Taylor."

His heart beat so loudly that he hoped she didn't talk for a moment or he wouldn't hear a word she said.

"Matt, you need to talk to Petey."

It took effort to concentrate on what she was saying. He wanted to be quiet and absorb the soft sound of her voice. It had only been a week, but he hadn't realized until now how much he missed her. "Petey?"

"He doesn't want to go to his baseball game. He's upset."

"About what?"

"You. He's upset that you stopped coming by— and well, I guess he saw you pack your tools this morning but you didn't come in to see him."

Matt mentally kicked himself. He'd gone to the house at five-thirty that morning to avoid seeing Petey, to be sure he wouldn't run into her. He hadn't considered how early Petey bounced out of bed. This morning he hadn't really been thinking about the boy, had he? All he'd been thinking about was himself, protecting himself. He'd never said goodbye to the boy. He'd thought that best. But when he was driving away this morning, he'd looked in his rearview mirror and had seen Petey standing in the driveway watching him.

"Matt?"

His gut clenched with the sound of Petey's voice. "Hey, Petey." He put a brightness into his tone that he didn't feel. "Why are you still home?" Matt glanced at the Little League calendar he'd tacked on the wall near his phone. "You've got a game this morning, champ."

"I don't want to go. You won't be there."

Damn, this was all wrong. "I got busy today. But I'll be there next time." It wasn't an empty promise. No matter how much it hurt him to see Petey, to see Taylor, he'd be there. He wouldn't let him down again.

"You will?"

"I'll be there." Matt mentally kicked himself. "Petey, go play your game. Okay?"

"Okay, Matt."

Tightly he held the phone to his ear. The silence went on forever before Taylor came back. "Thanks for talking to him."

"Yeah. Listen—"

"I won't bother you again."

"I was trying to be honest, to be fair to you." Who was he trying to convince? he wondered. Her or himself?

"If you don't mind, I won't say thank you."

Matt stood for a long moment before he realized she'd hung up. Hell, he'd wanted to end it so they'd parted as—what? Friends? That was impossible. He loved her. He loved both of them.

And he couldn't deny they'd had happy times. But those moments hadn't eliminated his bad memories, had they? That was his fault. He'd never allowed himself to forget the past. If he had, he would never have walked away from the two people who'd made his life feel complete again.

God, what had he done? He'd found the one he'd been looking for. And he'd let the past with Alisha blind him. Alisha. How could he have spoken Taylor's and Alisha's names in the same breath? he suddenly wondered. One woman had used him, the other had done nothing but give, even though she knew he would hurt her.

His confusion cleared. Nothing he'd believed or he'd felt before had anything to do with Taylor's money. There was another reason he hadn't let her love reach him, he realized suddenly. "Lock up when you leave." He snagged his car keys from the counter. "I'll see you later."

Smiling smugly, Cara held the fork in midair. "You have something to do?"

"I need to see if I can do some damage control." If he needed to sweet-talk, wheedle, grovel, he would. Once before he'd lost everything he'd thought he valued in his life. This time he'd gone in with the expectation that nothing could last, and now he realized he could have had it all.

Taylor had set aside her pride to call him. For Petey, she'd have done anything. She and Petey would get along fine without him, she believed. She didn't need a man in her life. She certainly wouldn't marry one just to give Petey a father, or get stuck with another one like Ian whose only interest was her money.

With some relief, as she came into the living room, she saw Petey dressed in his uniform and cap for baseball, waiting for her. Whatever Matt had said had worked. She was thankful to him for that. Though she didn't doubt Petey had more difficult moments to weather, in a small way, he'd begun the healing process.

She wished she had.

For his sake she plastered a smile on her face and cheered his team's efforts that afternoon at the baseball field. From now on, it would be only the two of them.

While driving home after the game, another win, she suggested to Petey that they make popcorn and watch his favorite video about the chimpanzee with a knack for getting into trouble. "In a few days, you'll have spring break. We could go to Disneyland. Would you like that?"

"Aunt Taylor, Matt sounded sad," he said suddenly.

She didn't want to know how he felt. She wasn't the one who'd thought they shouldn't be together.

"If he's sad because he's not with us, and we're sad because he's not with us, then why is he staying away?"

Taylor glanced away from traffic. He asked tough questions. "He thinks we're better off without him."

"That's silly."

Of course it was.

He twisted on the seat toward her. "If he said he was sorry, would you say okay?"

Another hard question.

"You love him, don't you?"

"Petey—"

He turned a penetrating stare on her, one that insisted on total truthfulness. "I love him, too."

She smiled at him, then negotiated the car onto the private drive. He insisted on honesty. How could she deny the truth. "Yes, I love him."

He just smiled, looking pleased, as if no problem existed.

In the house, still excited about the team's win, he rambled on about the game to Lottie. His elation didn't spread to Taylor. Her mood low, she walked to the study. For what seemed an eternity, she stood before the shelves of books. With a heavy sigh, she rested her forehead against one. How would she get past the feeling that something was missing?

Miserable, she didn't move.

She'd gotten along without him before, she reminded herself. She would again. But emotion hovered near, nearly choking her with the threat of tears.

Determined, she straightened her back. No tears, she demanded of herself and slid a book from a shelf. She couldn't give in to them.

A step from a sofa, she stilled as she heard a car engine. She wasn't expecting anyone. Frowning, in no mood for company, she wandered to the window. Not thrilled at having an uninvited visitor, she doubted she could play hostess believably.

The sight of Matt's truck stopped thoughts, stopped her heart. In less time than it took to draw a breath, her pride warred with her desire to rush outside. Pride won. She wouldn't go. She would send Leeland out to talk to him, find out why he was here.

That decision was snatched away during her next breath as she saw Petey racing across the lawn. Pressure swelled in her chest and promised to close off her windpipe when she saw him fly into Matt's arms.

Matt held the boy's sturdy body tightly to him. For a long moment he let his mind absorb the feel of the small hand at the back of his neck, the feel of him in his arms.

"I missed you, Matt."

"I missed you."

"We don't want you to go away."

We? He'd have liked to believe that meant Taylor

hadn't given up on him. But he tempered the hope trying to seize him.

Clinging to the boy, he sensed her before he turned and saw her slowly walking across the lawn toward them. She looked tired—and wary. Nothing was going to be easy, he guessed, even as he wished he could step close and take her in his arms.

"Matt came back, Aunt Taylor," Petey said brightly with her approach.

For Petey's sake, Taylor forced a friendly smile. "I thought you were done with the job."

Matt didn't doubt that the smile would disappear if Petey wasn't watching them. He heard no warmth, no softness in her voice. Well, if he had to, he would beg, he realized at that moment. "There's work still to do."

Work. This was all about the job? She couldn't handle this, she told herself. He'd hurt her badly.

Matt cursed himself. He didn't need to blunder the most important moment in his life. "Forget what I said." Groveling seemed a small price to pay. "That's not why I'm here." It occurred to him that he'd done the one thing so many others in her life had done—he'd let her down. "I didn't mean to hurt you, Taylor." He looked at Petey now. "Either of you," he said before setting him down.

Petey turned a smile that was bright and accepting up at him. "I believe you, Matt."

How forgiving the young were, Matt mused, touching the boy's shoulder. "Thanks, champ."

Taylor couldn't get the same words out.

"Your aunt and I need to talk, Petey. Okay?"

"Is this going to be mushy stuff?"

Real mushy, Matt hoped. He shrugged and waited while Petey dashed off toward the house. Then he made himself meet her stare. No warmth softened the blue in her eyes. No smile curved her lips. "I don't know how to explain. I really believed we wouldn't work."

Taylor shook her head and started to turn away.

"No second chances?" he asked.

She stopped immediately, closing her eyes. What was she doing? If she kept walking away, he wouldn't be leaving, letting her down. She would be pushing him away. Facing him, she kept her back straight, her body stiff. But she wasn't strong or resistant. With a few words this man could hurt her even more. "What happened wasn't about the differences in our lifestyles," she insisted, unwilling to accept what she knew wasn't true.

She really wasn't going to make it easy on him, Matt realized. "No, it wasn't," he admitted. He sighed in disgust at himself. How could he convince her that he wasn't a total jerk? "I made a mistake."

Taylor needed him to say everything. Without the words, she'd never believe they could have it all. "Because you didn't trust me to not be like her."

Matt struggled to explain what he'd only just realized. "You can cut me to ribbons right now. But I'm believing in us, trusting you to take me back even though I'm an idiot. If I didn't trust you, would I do that?" He wanted to open his arms to her, pull her close. "Who's lacking trust now?"

As she saw the regret in his eyes, her heart opened to him.

"I'm sorry. I wish I could wipe away all that happened between us." He saw a light come into her eyes, and knew then it hadn't been a mistake to come. "This wasn't about your money or different life-style. I kept backing away because I've been scared. If I got too close, I risked—" it took an effort to meet her gaze, hold it "—I risked losing again."

She tilted her head back to stare into his eyes. All the tenderness and love she felt for him filled her as she thought about how much he'd lost. How could she not remember the pain in his eyes when he'd talked about the baby?

Here goes, Matt mused. He had no choice but to say it all. "And I risked making a fool of myself again. None of this was about you," he tried to explain. "It was about me. Pride made me push you away because I didn't trust myself, my judgment. I made a mistake before, chose the wrong woman. I doubted myself, not you. I've been dumb. I've—"

Taylor raised a fingertip to his lips to silence him and save him from saying more. She didn't want him to beg.

"Taylor, I love you. I want promises. I want you and the boy in my life."

Love. She stopped breathing. He'd said *love*. The tears she'd managed to hold back before were smarting the back of her eyes. He'd never said those words before.

She made a small sound as he slipped his arms around her and buried his face in her hair. Silent, he simply held her, soaked in the feel of her close to him.

"I love you," she replied softly.

Relief coursed through him. "It's good you said that, because I'm not going anywhere. Now that I've stopped acting stupid you aren't getting rid of me." The need for her taste overwhelming him, he framed her face with his hands and kissed her hard, kissed her until he heard her soft moan. "We belong together," he said against her mouth.

"It sure took you long enough to realize that," she teased, still slightly breathless.

If he had any regret, it was that he hadn't believed that sooner. "Honey, what you see is what you get," he said, holding her tighter. "You know that, don't you?"

"What I see is the man I love," she assured him. An honest man, who worked hard whether it was pounding nails or artistically shaping wood into something beautiful.

Matt wondered what he would have said if she'd reconsidered. He laughed at himself. "There's something else."

"Could we quit talking?" Taylor murmured against his lips.

Matt chuckled at the pleasure in her eyes, the glow on her face. He moved his hands to her waist, then slid them around her slender back to draw her length snug against him. He heard the engine of a lawn mower, a plane flying overhead, the chirping of birds, but the world had narrowed to the space that separated them. "Just one more thing."

Leaning into him, she brought her lips close to his and sighed. "Just one more."

His eyes became serious. "After we're married, if Petey's for it, I want to adopt him. We all need to be—"

"A family," Taylor said softly, tears in her eyes. She hadn't thought it possible to love him more, but so much emotion flooded her that she thought she would burst with it. Coiling her arms around his neck, she pressed her mouth to his, doubting she would ever stop wanting the taste of his lips. No more words were needed. Here was the love she'd thought she would never find. Finally she really had all anyone could want.

* * * * *

Look for Jennifer Mikels's
engaging new romance,
FOREVER MINE,
coming in August
from Silhouette Special Edition.

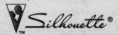

If you enjoyed what you just read,
then we've got an offer you can't resist!

Take 2 bestselling
love stories FREE!

Plus get a FREE surprise gift!

Clip this page and mail it to Silhouette Reader Service™

IN U.S.A.	**IN CANADA**
3010 Walden Ave.	P.O. Box 609
P.O. Box 1867	Fort Erie, Ontario
Buffalo, N.Y. 14240-1867	L2A 5X3

YES! Please send me 2 free Silhouette Special Edition® novels and my free surprise gift. Then send me 6 brand-new novels every month, which I will receive months before they're available in stores. In the U.S.A., bill me at the bargain price of $3.57 plus 25¢ delivery per book and applicable sales tax, if any*. In Canada, bill me at the bargain price of $3.96 plus 25¢ delivery per book and applicable taxes**. That's the complete price and a savings of over 10% off the cover prices—what a great deal! I understand that accepting the 2 free books and gift places me under no obligation ever to buy any books. I can always return a shipment and cancel at any time. Even if I never buy another book from Silhouette, the 2 free books and gift are mine to keep forever. So why not take us up on our invitation. You'll be glad you did!

235 SEN CNFD
335 SEN CNFE

Name	(PLEASE PRINT)
Address	Apt.#
City	State/Prov. Zip/Postal Code

Available July 1999 from Silhouette Books...

World's Most
Eligible Bachelors

AGENT OF
THE BLACK WATCH
by BJ JAMES

Black Watch

The World's Most Eligible Bachelor:

Secret-agent lover Kieran O'Hara was on a desperate mission.
His objective: Anything but marriage!

Kieran's mission pitted him against a crafty killer...and
the prime suspect's beautiful sister. For the first time in his
career, Kieran's instincts as a man overwhelmed his lawman's
control...and he claimed Beau Anna Cahill as his lover. But
would this innocent remain in his bed once she learned his
secret agenda?

**Each month, Silhouette Books brings you an
irresistible bachelor in these all-new, original
stories. Find out how the sexiest, most-sought-after men
are finally caught....**

Available at your favorite retail outlet.

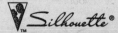

Silhouette®

Silhouette®SPECIAL EDITION®

LINDSAY McKENNA

delivers two more exciting books in her heart-stopping new series:

MORGAN'S MERCENARIES
III
THE HUNTERS

Coming in July 1999:
HUNTER'S WOMAN
Special Edition #1255

Ty Hunter wanted his woman back from the moment he set his piercing gaze on her. For despite the protest on Dr. Catt Alborak's soft lips, Ty was on a mission to give the stubborn beauty everything he'd foolishly denied her once—his heart, his soul—and most of all, his child....

And coming in October 1999:
HUNTER'S PRIDE
Special Edition #1274

Devlin Hunter had a way with the ladies, but when it came to his job as a mercenary, the brooding bachelor worked alone. Until his latest assignment paired him up with Kulani Dawson, a feisty beauty whose tender vulnerabilities brought out his every protective instinct—and chipped away at his proud vow to never fall in love....

Look for the exciting series finale in early 2000—when
MORGAN'S MERCENARIES: THE HUNTERS comes to
Silhouette Desire®!

Available at your favorite retail outlet.

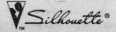

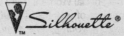

Silhouette SPECIAL EDITION

That SPECIAL *Woman!*

She's a wife, mother—she's you! And beside each Special Edition woman stands a wonderfully special man! Don't miss these upcoming titles only from Silhouette Special Edition!

❤❤❤

May 1999 HER VERY OWN FAMILY
by Gina Wilkins (SE #1243)
Family Found: Sons & Daughters

All her life, Brynn Larkin had yearned for a home—and a wonderful husband. So when sexy surgeon Joe D'Allesandro offered Brynn a helping hand—and made her an honorary member of his loving clan—had she finally found her very own family?

❤❤❤

July 1999 HUNTER'S WOMAN
by Lindsay McKenna (SE #1255)
Morgan's Mercenaries: The Hunters

Catt Alborak was ready for battle when she was thrown back together with Ty Hunter, the mesmerizing mercenary from her past. As much as the headstrong lady doc tried to resist her fierce protector, their fiery passion knew no bounds!

❤❤❤

September 1999 THEIR OTHER MOTHER
by Janis Reams Hudson (SE #1267)
Wilders of Wyatt County

Sparks flew when widowed rancher Ace Wilder reluctantly let Belinda Randall care for his three sons. Would the smitten duo surrender to their undeniable attraction—and embark on a blissful future together?

Look for That Special Woman! every other month from some of your favorite authors!

Available at your favorite retail outlet.

Silhouette ®

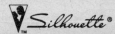